SCIENCE AND MAGIC

The Search Begins

Aditya Upadhaya

ISBN 978-93-90463-73-2

First published in India 2021 by Leadstart Inkstate
A Division of One Point Six Technologies Pvt Ltd

Sales Office:
Unit No.25/26, Building No.A/1,
Near Wadala RTO,
Wadala (East), Mumbai – 400037 India
Phone: +91 969933000
Email: info@leadstartcorp.com
www.leadstartcorp.com

Disclaimer: The views expressed in this book are those of the Author and do not pertain to be held by the Publisher.

Editor: Ateendriya Das Gupta
Cover: Jitendra Mahadik
Layouts: Victor Patali

Dedicated to all the dreamers and believers out there who have blessed this world with their grit and dedication. Never give up!!

Aditya Upadhaya, is an Electrical and Electronics Engineer by degree and a Software Engineer by profession with a fervour for writing. He is a Gold Medalist in his undergraduate studies. His profession gives him the opportunity to work in different places within India and abroad. His travels have introduced him to different cultures and traditions from all over the world. These experiences reflect on the characters of his book.

Aditya developed a habit of writing from a very young age and his first proper writing experience was a beautiful poem written for his crush. The poem however never reached his crush but instead, was discovered by his father many years later. This poem was the beginning that stirred the writing worms in his head, which eventually led him to discover his passion for writing. Aditya is also an amateur table-tennis player and dreams about owning a restaurant someday.

Science and Magic is Aditya's first book. Prior to this book, his passion for writing was not known by many. *Science and Magic* beautifully reflects his passion and his creative skills in fiction. Aditya has always believed that a writer can significantly impact someone's life simply by expressing their thoughts on paper. Writing lets one build a connection to readers and can inspire, motivate, and help them through their difficult days. He strongly believes that a good writer can help the audience challenge their imagination and think outside of the box. According to him, books are the best way to escape reality. There is no limit to your imagination and you can create a different, beautiful world for your readers. A good book can be used as a tool for entertainment, stress relief, and at the same time, for learning values and good deeds.

ACKNOWLEDGEMENT

To properly recognize all the people responsible for bringing me to this point in my life would take a considerable amount of space. Nevertheless, here is an attempt, mediocre at best, to recognize the individuals responsible for this book.

I would like to express my deep sense of gratitude towards my parents—my father, Mr Birendra Upadhaya, and my mother, Mrs Khira Bala Upadhaya—for rendering their full support and continuous love and care during the course of this work. Without their encouragement, I could not have written this book.

I will take this opportunity to thank Leadstart Publishing Pvt. Ltd for their trust in me by taking on the publishing duties for this book. It is their belief in my work that motivates me to write and produce better books.

Lastly, I would like to thank my editor, Ateendriya Gupta, and the entire team at Leadstart Publishing Pvt. Ltd for their continuous support and encouragement throughout the publishing process of this book. Their collective effort has led to this book being in the market.

Contents

CHAPTER 1

The Letter

Dear Jane, it's been long since I wrote to you … I couldn't be a good friend; I couldn't love you the way I wished to. I am trapped in this unrelenting web, and it will not let me go. We inquire into many mysteries, and if we do not find answers, if there are no answers—neither our technology nor our science can help us. I wish the human brain was not as curious as it is. Sadly, now the situation is such that it can only be us or them, and time is running out so fast. I feel so helpless here. The crew is almost gone. Only a handful of us remain. Before I say anything else, I want you to know that I love you and the kids. I may not survive this, but …

"Sam!"

A flash into time. Strange voices. They became clearer and clearer with every passing moment.

"Sam! We need you down here; our Triumph Guards have captured one of them. You've got to see this one."

Sam dashed downstairs, making his way through the circular stairs and a series of sealed rooms till he finally arrived at the detention hall. In front of him stood a beautiful girl. Her face glowed like the full moon, of which he had a rather distant memory, brown hair flowing till her feet, her pink eyes like a blooming lotus … she was barely able to stand, the Triumph Guards were holding her back tightly.

"She surrendered," the guards said, as if in response.

She seemed frightened. Sam noticed a deep wound on her right arm, with some strange markings on it. Somehow, he knew those marks, as if he had seen them before. Perplexed, Sam asked the guards to make her sit on the chair. She was held down, then clamped to one of the arms of the chair.

"I want to speak to her." Sam lowered his voice. "Alone."

The guards walked out.

Turning to her, he asked, "Who are you?"

"Help … me!"

"Help you? With what?"

She kept silent.

"What are those marks on your right arm? How did you get those wounds?"

"Help me."

Her voice was soft, barely audible.

"If you want me to help you, you have to answer my questions. Tell me who you are and where you've come from." He spoke loudly, snappishly.

The girl turned away, and the movement pulled at her hair, exposing her neck. There was a mark on the back of her neck: a black star, which seemed to be embedded into her flesh. Her flesh looked like it had been burnt multiple times to make that mark.

The symbol on her neck added to Sam's confusion. With a sigh, he said to himself, "Why do I feel as if I've seen this mark before?" The mark had shaken him. However, he controlled himself and continued to question her. "Why did you surrender?" He asked again, his voice suspicious. He paused for a few seconds, waiting for her to answer. "What is your purpose? Tell me!" He was yelling now.

"I don't want to die," she pleaded. "Please, help!" Her eyes had lost their light; she could barely keep them open. She kept muttering inexplicable cries for help. Suddenly, the dark grey wound on her arm began to glow. With every passing instance, it grew brighter and brighter, burning her flesh, the wound deepening. After a moment of what must have been excruciating pain, she fainted.

Sam tried to wake her up but it didn't work. He shouted, "I need help!" Mariane and John who were standing nearby rushed in. The two were Sam's helping hands, his best friends. People he loved and cared about. People he could count on.

Sam said, "We need to figure out her motive. Those marks on her arm and that black star—we need to find what they are. She is one of them. Which means that she is very important for this. We must study her well and find out everything we can. Will you guys take her to Research Meds? Keep her under observation. I will try to find out about the marks on her arm and neck." He snapped a few photos of the marks on her arm and on her neck. "Notify me if you learn anything. We don't know what is coming. Be alert." He waved as he was leaving.

Then, Sam headed towards the Library of Old and New. There, he would find Mr Hazelwood, popularly known as "The Keeper". He was an old man, with a rotund stomach and had an air of laziness. He sat on the keeper's chair reading books all day while stroking his white moustache.

Reaching the keeper's chair, Sam immediately pulled out his holographic ball and projected the photographs he had taken earlier. When Mr Hazelwood appeared next to him, he asked him about them. "What could these marks possibly mean?"

Mr Hazelwood leaned into the hologram, and his face turned pale. In the many years that Sam had known Mr Hazelwood, this was the first that Sam has seen him so worried and tense. Wiping the sweat off his forehead, the keeper spoke, slowly "These are ancient marks. They have not been seen in thousands of years. They symbolize a very dark power—once known to challenge all existence. To have found someone with these very markings means that someone has found out a way to use the power again."

After he had spent some time scouring the many selves of his library, he pulled out an old dusty book and said, "take this book and read it. You shall get what you seek. All your answers.'

"No one is safe. Not any longer," Mr Hazelwood pondered as he handed over the book to Sam.

Even more bewildered, Sam took the book and went to his quarters. For years, the book had lain untouched. The layer of dust on every page was testimony to everything it had seen, he thought. As Sam began to read, things started to fall into place. The mark on the neck of the girl, the black star, symbolized the dark matter of the universe. There existed a legend that the moment when time began its journey, both the god particle and dark matter were existent. One stood for life; the other, for destruction. Only one could win the rights to the universe. The god particle won, and so, life flourished in the universe. Dark matter had been disposed of into the unreachable corners of the universe. However, it still existed in some parts of the world, hidden from plain sight, waiting for someone to invoke it. And thousands of years ago, someone had done just that. They had found a way to put dark matter into the life created by god particles: the black star. Destruction ensued, as the life that was once a blessing could now be converted into a curse. Someone had to stop it. The dark matter was immensely powerful, and only a few species on whom the black star had been engraved could survive its power.

As he was leafing through the book, Sam received a call.

John's voice was shaky. "Sam! The girl is behaving strangely. She is screaming and shouting, and we are unable to control her. No sedative is working! The writings on her arm are glowing brighter and brighter. The star on her neck is almost eating up her flesh. I have never seen anything like this!"

"Hold on," Sam said, grabbing his coat. "I'm coming."

As he turned the lock to open his door, there was a huge explosion. Sam was flung away from the door. He lay on the floor of his room—wounded, unable to move. As his eyes blurred, he could see a burning figure approach, walking swiftly, as if the fire inflicted no pain. His eyes gradually closed. The last thing he saw was that everything around him was burning.

CHAPTER 2

The Academy

For centuries, humans, in their quest to achieve more, surpassed all boundaries that the Creator had set up for humanity's own well-being. In their greed, humans destroyed planets and stars, and pushed other creations to the point of extinction. In their bid to become the single-most dominant species in the universe, humans became blind and unjust, inflicting a lot of pain and suffering in the universe—not only on other creations but also on their fellow being. The human species became lost in its quest to control the entirety of creation.

Sam was among the many others who were a part of this exploration undertaken. They had set out to take humanity further, breaking all limits, and in the process, Sam, just a tall and skinny, smart and young scientist, discovered magical and mysterious worlds. But these worlds had their own secrets; some so dark that humanity was not yet ready to face them.

It all began when the human race had achieved everything it could have conceived of in the field of science. Humans realized that the universe was populated by others just like them. However strange it seemed, the universe had produced only one intelligent species, varying only in colour and build, residing in various nooks and corners of this vast universe. But the thirst of humans was unquenchable; they wanted answers even to the few questions that had been left unsolved. And with the entire species now united, they had begun to feel invincible and they turned to magic. They began their search for magical worlds—magical things and power spoken of only in legends. It was as if humanity, having achieved so much in science, after having set up its many colonies in the farthest regions of space, was now trying to return to a world that its scientists had once discarded and called impossible.

New research was done in the field of magic. Scholars submitted research papers on the powers of chi, black magic, superhuman powers, unicorns, powers of gods … the list was unending. Engineering and Information Technology were no longer considered subjects—nothing was left to be discovered! Now that the world had changed, people were considered intelligent and wise based on their knowledge about the unknown world: magic and mystery. They had begun to believe that a world must exist full of magical powers and magical creatures—in the same way that they had once assumed the existence of other planets with life. Humanity was returning to its primitive stages, and all believed in magic and mysterious powers and in an age before science. Debates ensued, although so such magical world had been found as yet.

Like Sam, many young minds participated in this race towards the discovery of magic. The best minds among them were funded by the coalition government to carry out their research in such fields. And Sam desired to one day be among them. He had attended the IMMR, the pioneer institution for studies and research on the existence of magical worlds—earlier known as Quanta and Space Exploration Agency (QSEA). It had first started out as a company that studied the element quanta in space and once was associated with deep-space exploration. After decades of space exploration and quanta research and development, with the emergence of the idea of a magical world, the institution turned towards other possibilities. Numerous manuscripts and ancient fossils had been found in distant space, and the institute changed drastically. It shelled out its shares to different governmental agencies and finally became the IMMR. Its objective had shifted completely. It now worked to further the research of magic and mystery. However, its key stakeholders were keen to look for new elements and to continue harnessing the possibilities of quanta.

After a long process, and tireless exploration through space and time, having collected enough ancient manuscripts and enough evidence to prove the existence of magic and various magical elements, the IMMR decided to introduce a field called "Magic and the Applied Sciences". Sam wanted to conduct further research on this very subject. After a tedious interview, Sam was called in to join the day after the interview results were declared. He was finally a part of the IMMR.

Sam and others like him would be the third generation of students to be part of the IMMR's programme. The academy was to nurture its students for a period of two terms over two years, both theoretically and practically, providing them with the hands-on experience required to work in the actual field. This academy was known as Volgarth. It was located at a secret location on a planet called Tiron. Volgarth accepted only the best students from across the universe and prepared them to take on the most challenging mission of finding a magical world, long lost from the face of the universe.

It took twelve hours to reach Tiron from Earth. Sam packed his bags immediately and set out. A Light Modular Vehicle (LMV) was awaiting him at the station nearest to his house, set to depart at 4 p.m. He boarded the vehicle and took off into the unknown. Twelve hours later, he could see vast structures on the surface of Tiron, each symbolizing the extent of humanity's desire to discover magical worlds. Tiron was a planet similar to the Earth but had been exploited to a lesser extent and still had dense and green forests; even the trees were much taller than trees are on earth. Tiron had huge mountains that stood like forts, guarding the planet's precious biodiversity. From the looks of it, Sam could not rule out the possibility of wild and strange animals existing in those forests.

The airfield at Tiron was quiet. It appeared damp appearance and contained few structures or even people. One huge building at the centre of the airfield was the only attraction in that place. As soon as he landed, Sam was accosted by a 7-foot tall bearded man with dark eyes, who did not appear to be from Earth.

"Welcome to Volgarth, Sam. I am Kasmuji from planet Eldor, and I will be your research guide. Please follow me."

Sam grabbed his bags and followed him. Kasmuji took him to a place that was simply called the "Dorm". It was located at the outskirts of the academy, and it could only be reached through narrow roads set like a maze. The paths were barricaded by huge walls, and on its top was a peculiarly blooming flower. The flowers were yellow and had the face of a monkey. Sam asked Kasmuji, "What are those flowers? I have never seen them before!"

"They are known as monkey orchids," Kasmuji replied. "This place is full of wonders. Don't be surprised if you see things you have never encountered before."

As they approached the dorm, Sam noticed that on one side of the wall were trees, a jungle of which soared high up to the skies. On the other side, he could see four pillars just as tall. "Why are there such dense trees on one side of the wall? What are those four pillars on the other side?" Sam asked.

"You ask a lot of questions. That is the forbidden forest. No one enters it. Those four pillars are known as the pillars of hope and are the foundation of this academy. They help us discover what we believe, looking through the entire universe. Don't you want to see what's inside those pillars? Of course you do. I'm right, aren't I? But don't worry. It will be long before you can get into those pillars, boy!" He laughed. "Ah! Here we are. Let me take you inside. This place is built for all the newcomers. Miss Hollande is the warden of this place. I am sure she will like you."

"Look around while I go and find Miss Hollande. There is so much to see here," said Kasmuji.

The dorm had a fresh feeling to it. They were to be received in a huge hall, which was packed with people, young minds who believed that the world to be much more than it seemed, in the existence of magic, in things that cannot be explained away by science. Men and women were alike, they had been granted admittance not based on their ethnicity, their native planet or gender, but based on their minds. The academy believed that the mind itself was a magical creation. All that scientific progress, yet not one race in the universe had been able to understand the mind and control its power.

The walls of the hall were resplendent with three-dimensional paintings of magical creatures only found in textbooks. It seemed lively out here. On one of the walls, strange but beautiful writing shone like gold. Sam had never seen the script before. As he gazed upon them in sheer astonishment, he heard a sweet voice from behind him.

"Don't they seem mysterious and beautiful? They are words of magic taken from ancient scrolls. Do you notice the golden colour? The writing turned to this sheen as soon as it was written on this wall. Nobody knows why. Doesn't it strengthen your belief in magic?"

Kasmuji had returned with a beautiful woman dressed in red. She was tall, fair and had straight hair that reached to her lower back. Her smile was as sweet as her voice. He said, "Meet Miss Hollande."

"Hello, Sam. I hope your journey went well. Welcome to the Dorm." She kept smiling at him. "I'm sure you had your surprises on the way. They all do. Don't feel awkward about it. You had already known that your beliefs would change when you decided to join our Academy right?"

"Yes, ma'am," Sam replied.

Her smile had not slipped. "As you can see, I have to attend to many like you and won't be able to show you to your room. Kasmuji will take you."

At that, Sam and Kasmuji headed away. They took the stairs to the hallway on the second floor. The hallway seemed to be never-ending. On both sides of the hallway were doors, which must have led to more rooms—an endless array of rooms it seemed like. On the way through the stairs, Sam noted that they were about three flights above him. The bars lining the stairs glowed a different colour every time someone touched them! After a while, they reached a door that had been left slightly ajar.

"This is your room. Please rest, I will come at ten to take you to the Forming Hall, where you will be addressed by our director. I expect he will ask you to form groups of three for you to study as a team. Pray that you get a nice group." Kasmuji smiled kindly as he left Sam in the room.

The room was nice. Through the window, the forbidden forest was visible in the distance. But the sun could be seen shining on the canopy. The dew on the trees reflected the sunlight, and it looked as if someone had lit thousands of candles that reached sky-high. It made the sky look orange and yellow. Sam stood near the window. *It is such a beautiful forest. Why would it be forbidden? What evil could possibly lurk in this sunshine?*

As Sam lay on the bed, many thoughts rushed through his mind. He had seen magic! He recalled the mystery of the road to the dorm, the faces of all those young minds, Kasmuji, Miss Hollande, his partners-to-be, and of course, what lay within those four pillars … Even though he was a student of the mystical sciences, he could not reason with the existence of a magical world. He had never expected to see what he had only encountered in books. He fell asleep dreaming of all the magic that awaited him …

At 9.00 a.m., Kasmuji came to take Sam to the Forming Hall. The path to the hall began with the same narrow mazes he had seen earlier. They walked until the maze opened to vast greenery. Magical, Sam thought. It was decorated with beautiful fountains, lush green gardens, trees in the form of unusual sculptures … As they walked into the space, Kasmuji asked Sam, "Do you believe in magic, boy?"

"Yes," Sam answered, "but not in the existence of a magical world."

Kasmuji looked askance at him and smiled, again that kind smile. "You will one day. But remember, you should first know where to find it."

"Have you found it?" Sam asked, excited.

"Yes, yes I have. Everyone understands magic differently. For me, it is where my heart lies—my home. I see magic in my home, in my people. But I am here because I believe that there is magic in all of us, that we just need to know where to look for it."

Sam did not quite understand Kasmuji. As they walked further, Sam saw a huge building, so huge that you could not see beyond it. The four pillars stood, one in each of the four directions guarding the structure. Like bodyguards guarding their king. It looked like a castle so gigantic that all the kings could have lived in it together. Those pillars seemed even larger than they had earlier!

"Is this the Academy?" Sam asked.

"Yes. Isn't it huge? This is where you are going to learn all that you desire. You will find your place in the world of magic. Don't be so shocked ... it's only just begun. There is much, much more inside," Kasmuji said.

As they stood at the door of Volgarth, Sam was astonished at how vast it was. It was the biggest institution Sam had ever seen. Standing on the doorstep, as he looked up, it seemed that it kept growing. He was excited to look inside and learn its secrets. As they entered the building, he saw a hall that had a similar atmosphere to the one at the Dorm, except much larger. The hall opened to four corridors in four directions, each of them long and dark. Who knew where these corridors lead to? The walls of the hall had similar scripts and writing like at the dorm. Sam recognized words of magic taken from ancient books. They shone like gold. The paintings looked more real now. A realization dawned on him: Volgarth was a place full of mystery and magic. There were so many questions now in his mind. He wanted to know so much about this place.

"I am going to learn everything about this place," he promised himself.

"This is the Great Recep Hall," Kasmuji said. "It is the first thing every newcomer sees in this place."

On the door, they were greeted by someone.

"He is the Gatelocker." Kasmuji pointed towards a dwarf-like man who stood at the entrance, a few steps inside the building. "He protects us. He is the first line of defence of this building. In case an enemy someday attempts to break in. Don't go by his size, Sam. He is a master of Therise, an ancient fighting technique. Only three people in the universe know this technique. He can single-handedly defeat a thousand soldiers in one go."

Sam had so much to ask about this Gatelocker. *Who is he? Where does he come from? What is Therise? How did the dwarf learn such a rare art? Why does such a big institution have only one dwarf guarding its entrance?* Yet, he only said, "It is news to me that the IMMR has enemies. Why would they try to enter Volgarth? All they will find here are scholars!"

Kasmuji winked, "Yes, the IMMR has enemies. Both the IMMR and Volgarth are so much more than you think it is. You will learn in time, boy."

Sam felt goosebumps on his arms. A feeling of mystery pervaded this place. Only his first day, and already, there was so much he didn't know! What had he learned all these years, the universe is so much more than what its inhabitants imagine.

Kasmuji stopped to chat with an old friend, and Sam was left to look around for himself. The hall started to fill with other scholars like him—newcomers—most of whom shared his confusion, most of whom were trying to figure out the mysteries. As Sam looked at them, he saw how lost they were in thought, their eyes disbelieving. He saw a young boy. His eyes were as calm as that of Kasmuji. Surprisingly, he did not look awed by what he had seen so far. He had blue eyes and had curly black hair. For a while, Sam was sure that he was not a newcomer. Sam approached him and asked, "You don't seem to be surprised by the mystery of this place. Are you new here?"

The boy gave him a stern look. "Yes, I am a newcomer," he said rudely as he walked past Sam.

"Well … that did not go as planned," Sam uttered softly. It was as if the boy was hiding something, some secret deep inside him. Deep in thought, he heard Kasmuji call, "Sam!"

"Sam, meet Mr Esdorg. He is an old friend and a resourceful person to know at Volgarth."

"Hello, young fella. I will be meeting you here quite often." Mr Esdorg was a middle-aged man, with a scar on his right cheek. One of his eyes seemed artificial and made of marble. He always had a smile on his face.

Probably to hide how scary his face is, Sam thought.

They now entered the corridor facing the east. "This is where the magic starts." Kasmuji gave Sam a pat on the back as they moved forward.

The corridor was filled with beautiful paintings of men, women, nature—paintings that appeared simple, just like what he had seen on earth. The atmosphere of the Great Recep Hall did not seem to linger here. There was no magic in those paintings. The flowers in the vases were lilies and roses and jasmines. Nothing magical about them. So normal, unlike what Sam had seen till now. He was confused. In a doubtful tone, he asked Kasmuji, "You said that this was where the magic starts—but there is no magic here. It's so simple in this corridor. I don't understand. The hall seems to be so full of magic, but the corridor is so devoid of it. Why?"

Kasmuji could see the disappointment in Sam's eyes. He knew what it was like for those new to this world. It must be confusing for him. He put a hand on Sam's shoulder and said, "I know this is hard on you, Sam. But remember, everything you see is not real. Reality is usually very simple, and the greatest magic is real. So, this is where the magic starts. In your time, you will see many unbelievable things. But always remember, you will find the greatest magic hidden in the simplest of things."

The goosebumps returned to prick Sam's neck. He understood. And the smile returned to his face.

The corridor branched off this way and that, left and right, towards halls and classes and laboratories. The Forming Hall was located somewhere where it branched off, the fourth of its branches towards the left. When they reached, Sam saw that the hall was a beautiful place. Its floors were white marble and beautiful flowers hung from the ceiling at the edges of the hall. Paintings of all the former directors and the present director of Volgarth adorned the walls. There were also paintings of ancient planets—planets known to be the birthplace of life itself. Sam had studied about these planets. Interesting statues representing ancient mystical beings were lined around the hall. Statues of talking birds, three-eyed men, horses that had wings, angelic women … and many others. Sam knew that these statues had been kept there for a reason, but he didn't know what that reason was.

As all the new and old scholars, staff, teachers and guests gathered inside the hall, the director got on the stage. He was a tall person with a hood over his head, and his face was hidden. Sam had heard earlier that the identity of the director was kept secret from the new scholars. The murmurs stopped as the director began to speak.

"Everyone! My name is Soldon and I am the director of Volgarth. It is my privilege to welcome you all to another year in the IMMR's Volgarth. For years now, we have been trying to discover the magical world, a world that is still a mystery to us—despite our advances in science. You will be seeing the fruits of our labour as you progress in this Academy. Every year, this yield increases. We discover more and more, and it brings our proposed magical world closer to reality. You all see the statues around you. Most of you are familiar with these mystical beings, have heard stories about them, read about them in books. We display these statues on this day for a reason. We want to give our new scholars a goal that guides them towards what we are all looking for. In your days in this Academy, and for the rest of your life, these creatures should be real to you. They should exist somewhere in this universe, and your goal in life should be to find them. You cannot find something that you don't believe in. This is what we teach you here—to believe. I assure you, your work is not going to be in vain. We want you to have a reason to dedicate yourselves to your work, to inspire you. All this can only come through belief. You must believe that such a world is out there. This is the first thing that you need to do. Until you believe, you will not be able to proceed further. So dear scholars, from this day onwards, start believing. Some of you have already met your guides, the others will meet them in a short while. It is now time to let the new scholars know their groups! Each group will have three members and one guide. I now ask my colleague, Mrs Lassslie, to please announce the groups."

Groups started being announced. Sam already knew his guide Kasmuji. Now, Sam would also know who his fellow scholars were. It was time to form Kasmuji's group. Sam's name was called first, followed by another girl and a boy, Mariane and John. Mariane had straight brown hair and blue eyes, while John was well-built, dark-brown eyes and short hair. A total of ten groups were formed. Afterwards, Kasmuji took his group and went to the west corridor of the building, to the Chamber of Learning. This corridor housed all the learning chambers of all the scholars, both old and new. Their chamber was the fourth one on the corridor according to their group number, and it had its own library, dining hall, cubicles for the scholars and yet another room. Kasmuji took them directly to the common area and sitting there, began to speak.

"This is your group's discussion room. You will do all your research and study here. Our library is separate and will provide all the books you require. You will spend your entire day in this building. When you don't have classes and are not scheduled time in the laboratories—that is in your free time—you will be in this chamber. All you need will be provided. Food will be brought here in a timely manner from the dining halls. You have also been given separate cubicles and may conduct your individual studies there. I do hope you will feel comfortable here. I will leave you guys to get to know each other. But your work starts from tomorrow. I will come at 9 a.m."

Other than this overwhelming space, Kasmuji also showed them a secret door, which directly opened on to an underground path leading to the Dorm. They were strictly instructed to use only this path to reach their rooms.

"You are now a part of Volgarth, but you are still new to this place. Remember that you are not allowed to go through the path you came from, the one leading from the Dorm. Only use this path," Kasmuji said as he closed the door to the secret path and left.

As Sam, Mariane and John sat together and spoke to each other, Sam learned that Mariane was enrolled in Medical Sciences, John in Technical Sciences, while he was in Magic and Applied Sciences. All three of them had come from Earth.

CHAPTER 3

Friends

It was 1 p.m. and Sam, Mariane, and John were still in their chambers getting to know each other. They were discussing their parents.

Mariane's parents were doctors, both of whom worked for the Advanced Medical Research Institute on Earth. She had grown up lonely and neglected, as her parents had never been home. "I always knew that they had a good reason for it, that they ultimately wanted to make the universe a better place. But sometimes, years would pass before I saw them," she grumbled. Her aunt, Ms Marie, had taken care of her as a child. Being rather studious, she had few friends and only one dream—to join the IMMR in Volgarth. "I gave everything I had to reach here. I have something to find out."

Immediately, Sam had an inkling that she too had a secret. Sam could always tell if someone was hiding something. But, on seeing her face, he understood that she would not be revealing it today. So he did not ask.

John had illustrious parents—a mother who was a teacher of engineering at the International Engineering Institute and a father who was a pilot for Titean, the mothership of the IMMR. In fact, he was the captain of the ship! John had lived with his mother and had always had her by his side. Although he hardly saw his father, his mother made sure that he never felt his absence. He spoke in a manner that made it apparent that he had had many friends since his childhood and that he had never been alone. During school, since he failed to pass muster in front of his father, John was humiliated and mocked in front of his father's colleagues. He wanted to prove his dad wrong, and this desire had driven him to pursue Technical Sciences and join Volgarth. He had not spoken to his father in two years. "I promised myself that I would meet him only after I have proven myself completely," he said.

"You should speak to him. He's your father, I'm sure he'd never wish you ill—despite how he scolds or mocks you," Sam said.

John appeared dismayed. "You don't know a thing, Sam."

Sam stopped pushing. He understood that their relationship must be complicated and decided to not say a word.

"Hey!" Mariane broke the awkwardness. "What about your parents, Sam?"

The smile faded from Sam's face. But to Sam's relief, before he could respond, the Chamber door opened and two people entered, taking long strikes. An old lady and a young man. They came into the discussion room.

"Hello, young fellas. I am Ginger," the woman spoke. Pointing a finger at the man, she continued, "And that's Solemon. We're here to discuss your meals."

"Meals are provided twice a day, to be eaten in the dining room. Fruits and snacks are available round-the-clock, in case you feel hungry. Now, if you will, please come with us. We will show you to the dining room. It's time for lunch," Solemon said. They proceeded towards the dining hall. As soon as they entered the dining hall, their eyes lit up in awe of the place. The dining hall was like none Sam had ever seen. It was almost as if it had no end. There was a large balcony adjoining the dining hall, which overlooked the valley below. It also had a separate section for staff on the first floor, which had a small platform overlooking the entire dining hall. As Sam walked through to sit at his place, he couldn't help but notice the old rustic charm of the dining hall. With wooden chandeliers hanging from the ceilings and a series of old wooden tables and chairs laid perfectly in sync, the dining hall seemed straight out of a fairy tale. It had large windows the height of five men running across the dining hall on all sides, which gave a beautiful yet mysterious view of the forest and valley outside. Salient fireflies lit up the whole hall, and yet there was no disturbance to the meal services going on. Each table had a rotating belt that carried all the food in circles.

As the students sat down, they could hear the clinking sound of glasses. Curious, everyone looked towards the direction of the sound. They could see Ginger and Solemon standing up on the platform adjoining the staff section, ready to address the mass. "This is your dining hall, Lyceum. It serves as the only dining hall in Volgarth for both students and staff. I hope you enjoy your meal. Now let us pray before we start our meal," Ginger said.

As everyone present there started praying, Sam had a strange thought pondering his mind. This was the first time he was involved in praying. This was completely new for him. The idea of something which was discarded long before by science. As the prayers continued, he wondered, in this universe where science is everything, does the idea of God still exist? His mind could not make immediate peace with the prayers unlike most of the students present there. For them, this was the first step into finding the magical world. The idea of God. Or did the prayers symbolize something else?

As soon as the prayers ended, food was served. As the belts on the table started to spin, food started coming in. It was a feast. Considering the conditions Sam came from, the food felt royal. There was every kind of food that Sam knew and more. Much more! As the students started munching on the delicacies, they heard a voice coming from the same platform.

"We'll return soon. You'll have eaten your fill in an hour, I presume?" Ginger said, and both her and Solemon came down the spiral stairs and left the dining area.

As they ate, John restarted their earlier conversation. "Sam, we were talking about your mom and dad, weren't we?" Sam stopped.

He put down his fork. "I don't know them. I've never seen them. I am an orphan," he said, careful to not let his grief show.

"Oh Sam! I'm so sorry, I had no idea," John immediately cut in.

"Don't apologize. It's not your fault," Sam said softly and turned back to his meal. Soon, Ginger and Solemon came back and took away their dishes. As they parted, Ginger said, "We hope you have enjoyed your first lunch here."

They all murmured noises of assent. "Yes, it was grand."

"I'm full. I think I will go to the dorm and rest," John said as they left.

"Wait, wait. I'm coming too. Sam?" Mariane called out and turned to Sam.

"Yes, of course. Tomorrow is a big day, and I'm already tired today. I need a lot of rest. Let's go."

They opened the door to the secret passage and went inside it. It opened directly onto the stairs, about one flight of it underneath them. After climbing down, they came across a straight path lit by fireflies. It looked magical.

"This path is the one Kasmuji talked about. It should lead us to the Dorm. What did he say again—'follow it straight and do not take any turns'?"

As they set off on the path, they saw several other paths branching into the main path. But the path they walked on remained straight and narrow.

"These other paths must be for the other new scholars for their own chambers," Mariane reasoned, and the boys nodded.

They came across a door down the path. It had ominous lettering on it. "Don't trespass here. Stay away."

"What's behind that door?" Sam asked.

"I don't know," John replied, "but it clearly states that we should not try to find out."

Sam had always been a curious boy. Sometimes, his curious impulses were such that he couldn't even control them. He moved to see what was behind that door. His friends shouted out, "Sam! Where are you going? Are you mad? It's our first day here. We cannot trespass where we're told not to. Come back!"

"You guys stay back." He turned to reassure them. "But I want to know what's behind this door. It is my curiosity that has brought me here, and I cannot let my curiosity go. I am going in."

He turned and began to walk towards the door. Surprisingly, he heard footsteps approaching him. Mariane and John were following him!

"We're partners, aren't we? Someone has to watch your back. Let's go in together. On the count of three, open the door," John said, winking at Sam.

"One … two … and three!" they chorused.

It had turned into a night of merriment. Sam had begun to like John.

Sam's fingers were on the knob of the ominous door, but as he began to twist it to open it, his hands were grabbed and pulled away. Had they been caught? They looked around in fear.

To their astonishment, they saw a boy—a new scholar like themselves. Sam recognized him. "I met you earlier!" he exclaimed.

"I know that," the boy snapped. "What are you so happy about? Don't you guys know where to go and where not? You touch that knob again, and the director is going to learn of it the next moment. Do you guys want to be expelled?"

Terror struck their hearts on hearing his words, and they backed away from the door. The idea of the director learning of their mischief and expelling them was too much to take! They turned to leave the mystery door behind and proceed. The boy had already walked ahead of them. Sam shouted, "Hey! I'm Sam. What's your name?"

"I don't tell strangers my name," the boy replied without turning around.

The three shrugged at each other. The end of the path led upwards, a flight of stairs that ended at the reception hall of the dorm.

As they reached, they were addressed by Miss. Hollande. "Welcome back! I hope your first day at Volgarth went well. You may now proceed to your rooms. You will be served tea in the evening. You'll have to come down to the dining hall to get it, however. It's at 5 p.m. Don't forget," she said with the same sweet smile on her face.

John turned to Sam. "Which one is your room?"

"205. What's yours?" Sam asked.

"Oh! That's good. Mine is room 206, the adjacent one. What's yours, Mariane?" John asked.

"Mine is in the girl's section, on the first floor. Room 105," Mariane replied.

"Had we already been grouped together?" Sam said.

"What do you mean?" Mariane said to him.

"I think, John and I have adjacent rooms … and your room is the one right below mine. That makes me doubt …"

"Oh! Please, Sam, stop your curious mind for once. We're tired. Go rest. We will see you at tea," Mariane mocked Sam as she left for her room.

"Come on buddy, let's go." John put a hand on Sam's shoulder, and they both went off.

But doubt had entered Sam's mind. He would not be satisfied without clearing that doubt. Sam lay on his bed and closed his eyes, thinking about everything that had happened that day … the closed door, the coincidence of all three members of his group getting the rooms that they got … he was asleep before he knew.

"Sam!" Someone was screaming. "Sam!"

As he opened his eyes, he saw two foggy figures standing right before him. He quickly leapt off his bed. The two figures guided him down the stairs, through the reception hall, out of the building. Sam followed them as the screaming voices grew louder in his head.

The figures led him through the road through which he had come in with Kasmuji. Finally, the two figures stopped. Sam looked around him and saw the forest. It was daylight but the forest appeared dark, little to no light entered through the tall trees. The only thing bright there were the two figures. Sam knew immediately that it was the forbidden forest, the one he could see from the window of his room. He stood there and shouted out to the figures, "Who are you and why are you screaming so much? What has happened?"

But he received no reply. Only the screaming. The sound grew louder and shriller. It was so piercing that Sam screamed out, "Stop, please stop."

He knelt on the ground holding on to his ears, begging the screaming to stop.

When he raised his head, something else was there. A dark shadow behind the two bright figures. As the dark shadow came closer, it seemed to grow, the brightness of the two figures diminished slowly. Soon, it seemed like the shadow had engulfed the bright figures. The screams became even louder. Sam did not know what those screams were, but their sound was so high-pitched that Sam felt as if his head would explode. He could not take it anymore. His eyes turned red as if on the verge of exploding. The dark shadow was now everywhere. The forest was much darker. He could see nothing there. Only a voice …

Knock knock, knock knock … someone was knocking at a door.

"Sam! Sam! Wake up, man. It's time for tea. It's almost 5 p.m. Sam?"

As Sam opened his tightly shut eyes, he realized that it had all been a dream. It was John at the door, his fellow scholar. The fear still clutched at him. Sam jumped out of his bed and looked at the mirror. His eyes were not red. His face was sweaty, however. He looked out of the window and saw the forbidden forest. Thoughts flashed through his mind …

"I am coming." He pulled on his shirt. "One sec," he said to John as he wiped off the sweat and went to open the door.

"You slept for a long time, Sam," John said, his eyes concerned.

"Well, I was a bit tired," Sam replied. He didn't want to tell John about the dream.

They walked down to Lyceum together. On the first floor, they were joined by Mariane. The other new scholars were already seated at long tables. It was five minutes past 5 p.m. They scanned the area for a seat, but the hall was packed. Then, they found a table that was almost empty. Only one guy. The same guy they had met at the secret passage, the one who had stopped them from opening that door. Steadily, they rushed to the table and found his head bowed, reading a book. He looked stern, and they were hesitant to ask him if they could sit with him. Sam ventured, "Hi, can we share the table with you? There's no other seat left."

The boy looked up, and then around, as if to check if Sam was lying. There really was no more space. He nodded, at which they quickly grabbed a chair each and sat down. The silence was awkward. John, who was not accustomed to such quiet, decided to break the ice.

"Hi, I am John," he held out his hand to the boy. The boy ignored it. He looked sternly into his book. John tried again, "I'm John. May I know your name?"

The boy closed his book, gave him a harsh look and said, "I am Jonathan. Don't ask me anything else."

His manner shocked them. Exchanging looks, they silently agreed that it would be better for them to not force him to speak further. As the three turned to each other to resume their conversation, they heard the clinking sound of glass.

It was Miss Hollande. She was standing on the dais on one side of the dining hall, clinking her glass with a knife. She began to speak.

"Hello, my dear new scholars. It is my privilege to host you all this evening. I hope you have had a great time at Volgarth today. Some things here may have left you a little shocked, but you must make a habit of it. The things that you are going to see in the course of your stay here will be far more surprising, and most of those things will have no explanation. This is why you all are here, to find explanations and unexplainable things. Getting into Volgarth is tough, and those who have made it are all special. I would like all of you to know that your stay here will not be easy. You will receive great care, but you will also be pushed to your limits. So, be prepared. Here, every moment will be a surprise. This dorm, Volgarth … all these places are filled with mysteries you have not even imagined. Some of them are real mysteries set up by the founders of this place and others have been set up to test your skills. Beyond Volgarth, you all will be working in the vastness of this universe. So, you have to be prepared. You should work as a team. Build relationships—not only with your group members but also with the other students. Utilize every moment wisely. Having said this, you may now turn to your tea, get to know each other. Dear students, go ahead and make friends!"

The silence of the dining hall broke as Miss Hollande ended her speech. Everyone started to interact with one another. The tea went cold on some tables. There were so many people here.

Sam turned to Jonathan again; this time he was curious. "Why are you alone? Where is your group?" Surprisingly, Jonathan was more polite.

"I prefer to stay alone and don't like groups. But if you are so interested, they are sitting there. The second table."

Impulsively, Sam rose from his seat and walked towards them. He was intent on talking to more of the students. "Hey, I'm Sam. I am from Kasmuji's group. We are sitting there with one of your mates, Jonathan. Would you like to come over and join us?"

They agreed, and there was a shuffle of cups and plates as they walked to the table where Jonathan sat. As soon as Jonathan saw his group mates there, he turned red and angry.

"Why did you call them here? I told you that I don't like groups. I should not have allowed you guys to sit with me here." He stood up and left the dining hall, his book still in his hand.

At this outburst, one of his group members piped up. "Don't mind him, guys, he is a little absurd at times," he began. "I'm Juliana. From Marth. That's Jason, and he's also from Marth," she said pointing towards her other group mate.

"And … that was Jonathan. whom you have already met. He is also from Marth. He is a bit arrogant but has a heart of gold. He's seen too much. Don't mind him."

"No, no, nothing like that. We don't mind. Don't worry," Mariane said. "So, how was your first day?" she asked Juliana.

"Oh! It was wonderful. We had no idea about so many of these things. Our chambers are spacious and our guide, Mr Esdorg, is a wonderful man. We have beautiful rooms with good views. What else can you ask for?" Juliana remarked. "How was yours?"

"Oh! More of the same. Seen a lot of …"

Sam interrupted to ask Jason, "Jason, what are your group's room numbers at the dorm?"

"Mine is 256, Juliana's is 156 and Jonathan's is 257," Jason replied.

"You see, guys! I told you that there was something going on with our room patterns. It's not a coincidence," Sam exclaimed.

"Oh! Mr Curious again. Stop dissecting everything. There is nothing mysterious about our room patterns," Mariane mocked Sam.

Sam quietened down, but the doubt had grown in his mind, and he was more suspicious than ever. Something fishy was going on with their room patterns.

As time passed in the dining hall, they spoke and learnt the names of many more groups. There were scholars from all corners of the universe. This felt magical to Sam. So many people! He felt something in his heart, a feeling that he could not explain at that moment. He felt as if he understood a little of Kasmuji's words, when he had said, "I see magic in my people." It was the bond shared by each of them there, with one another as living beings, the sense of responsibility for one another, that felt like magic. Tea had barely taken any time, but they all already had nicknames and personalities.

Sam, the curious; Mariane, the bookworm; John, the determined; Jonathan, the arrogant; Juliana, the mature; Jason, the funny; Krilon, the fighter; Sammer-the-hammer; Jane, the beauty; Canny Jenny; fat Richard; Reagel, the cook …

So many new acquaintances in one day! It was like a dream for Sam, an orphan, who had hardly seen any joy, who had no family. All these people suddenly meant something akin to family. People whom he cared about and who cared about him. He was not just seeing magic—he was living in it.

CHAPTER 4

Second Day

They returned to their rooms after tea a couple of hours later. Dinner was to be served at 9 p.m. in the same place, but now, the scholars had been asked to prepare for their classes the next day. They would also be briefed then.

Sam sat at his table to study, but he could not stop himself from wonder about all the things that he had experienced. Those walls, the flowers on the top, the four pillars, those long corridors, the chambers, the secret passage, the mystery of that door, the room pattern ... many thoughts passed through his mind. His curiosity had been thwarted, and he felt frustrated that he did not have the answer to so many questions. He sat idly at the table, wondering about the mysteries that Volgarth held.

And his friends had revived a long-forgotten question. An orphan should want to learn about their parents. Who were they? Why did they abandon him? The thought of meeting them someday brought tears to his eyes.

Gathering his thoughts, his eyes glanced at the window, and he again noticed the forbidden forest. It was the night of a full moon and the top of the trees glowed like a blanket of light. Suddenly, San remembered his dream. Something in his dream had taken him into that forest. The screams began to haunt him again. *But it's not a dream this time*, he thought. The more he stared at the forest, the louder the screams grew. He found himself forming a whimper, then a scream.

"—stop, please, stop," he was begging.

John must have heard, for he rushed into Sam's room. But the door was locked. Sam's screams were horrific. John felt helpless as he kept turning the doorknob to the locked room. He could not even open the door. Determined to help, he ran downstairs and notified the first person he saw.

Miss Hollande.

The screams were loud enough to reach the girls' section on the first floor. By the time Miss Hollande reached Sam's door, all of them accumulated near the door. She had to push through the crowd. Kasmuji and Mr Esdorg were with her. As Kasmuji tried to push the door and open it, he knew it was locked and they'd have to break it.

"We need to break the door immediately," he said with concern in his eyes.

Both Miss Hollande and Mr Esdorg saw immediately the concern on Kasmujis eyes and agreed to break the door without wasting any time.

As the onlookers looked in horror, the three of them recited a spell before Kasmuji kicked the door with all his force—breaking it open.

When they entered the room, Sam lay in a corner, holding his head and screaming—words that no one understood. As they near him, he looked up at them. His eyes were swollen. They had turned a deep red.

The crowd drew back, frightened. Kasmuji and Esdorg took hold of him and placed him on the bed. But all Sam could see was a dark shadow. It was engulfing all his friends. They were all screaming for help.

"Help us, Sam. Please. Help us." The same words, over and over. They vibrated in his ears. Sam felt helpless. He could not even move. Aware of the guides around him, he found words to cry out. "What is happening to me?" he screamed. "No! Please don't. Don't take them," he was begging now, speaking to the shadow, his surroundings forgotten. The shadow kept engulfing everyone. It had reached Kasmuji, who seemed to be saying something. His words were soft and barely audible over the screams.

"You are much more than you think, Sam," Kasmuji's last words were engulfed by the shadow within itself.

His breath caught in his throat, he watched helplessly as the shadow approached him. And then, all at once, his eyes flew open. He was breathing—heavily, but breathing. Sweat dripped from his entire body as if he had taken a shower. His clothes were drenched in sweat. He had fallen asleep at his table while staring at the forests. He looked at the clock by his side. It was 8.55 p.m. hours—time for dinner. *Another dream?* He quickly got up from his table, changed out of his dripping clothes, wiped off the sweat from his body and went out of his room. John was already outside. On seeing Sam, John said, "Oh! I was just about to knock at your door."

Sam could not pay attention to John's words. The dream had taken a toll this time around. The sweat still dripped down his body. He could feel it.

"Are you all right, Sam?" John asked.

"I am fine. It's just the heat, it's making me sweat. Don't worry." Sam faked a smile. His mind was still stuck in the dream. *Why he was having these dreams*, he wondered. This was a first. He'd never been this accosted by nightmares before.

Questions tangled into each other as he walked to dinner.

What is this dream? Does it have something to do with Volgarth? I've never had these dreams before …Who were those bright figures? That black shadow … Why were the people I care about vanishing into the darkness?"

All these questions had clouded Sam's mind in such a way that he hadn't even realize that they had reached the dining hall.

"Hey! Sam! Is everything okay?" Mariane asked him, drawing him out of his reverie.

"Oh. When did you join us, Mariane?" Sam asked in astonishment.

"Look at that. Which wonderland are you in, Sam? I have been here for ten minutes now." Mariane laughed. Sam didn't join in on the joke—he couldn't. The questions and the events of the nightmare kept running through his mind, again and again. He hadn't even realized that he had taken someone else's plate. He walked towards a table.

"Hey! Excuse me! Sam, you took my plate."

Sam heard a sweet voice calling him from behind. As he turned to look, he saw that it was Jane. She had been rightly dubbed a "beauty".

"Oh!" He looked at his hands, holding her plate. "I am extremely sorry, Jane. I didn't mean to." They exchanged their plates.

"Don't be too lost on your first day." Jane smiled at him.

As Sam returned to his table with his plate, he was blushing red. Seeing him, Mariane teased, "Look who is blushing. Someone brought a nice plate with him today. Was your wonderland made up of her, Sam?" She laughed.

John joined in on the joke and tried to pull Sam's leg. His seat was sitting facing Jane's table. As Sam arrived, he quickly vacated his seat and gave it to Sam. "Sit here Sam, you won't need to go to a wonderland now, will you?" Although he was aware of his surroundings now, and slightly distracted, he was still consumed by his nightmare. He would have usually replied with sarcasm. But now, he simply smiled and sat down.

On seeing this, Mariane and John stopped laughing. John turned his head towards Mariane and whispered, "He wouldn't have sat here so calmly after all our teasing, would he? I feel like something is off."

"Yes, I too think so, but … should we ask? Do you think he will tell us?" Mariane whispered back.

Sam saw them whisper among themselves. He hadn't noticed but Jonathan stood behind him. He leaned in, slightly surprising the already confused boy and whispered into his ear, "I know why you are tense. Those dreams, right?"

Sam was shocked to hear that from Jonathan. How had Jonathan known about the dreams? He asked, "How … what?" He couldn't figure out the right words. "Who are you?"

Jonathan straightened. He had just as abruptly returned to his arrogant posture. Smiling, he said, "You will know when it's time."

The questions now ate at Sam. He couldn't even complete his meal.

A voice spoke at his back as the scholars all finished their meals. "Are you all right, Sam? You did not finish your meal." It was Miss Hollande.

"Ma'am, I am not that well," Sam replied.

"Oh! What happened? Will you be fine, or do you want to see a doctor?"

"I'll be fine, ma'am. Just need some rest."

"All right dear, go get some sleep now. You've had a tiring day. Try to sleep, no matter how stressed you are." Miss Hollande left with these words.

All the newcomers left the dining hall and went to their rooms. As Sam lay in his bed, sleep eluded him. He was afraid he'd have the same dream. It was only his first day in Volgarth. Along with everything else, his own life appeared mysterious to him now. As the night passed, Sam lay on his bed, tossing from one position to other, wondering what was going on. He sat up, then stood, then he paced from one end of the room to the other. He could not sleep. It was as if that shadow had engulfed his sleep.

It was two in the morning. While Sam was pacing, two others were awake. In the reception hall, two people wearing hoods were talking about Sam.

"It has started. The dreams have begun."

"It means the time is not far."

"Yes, but it's still the first day of the dream."

"I know. We must be careful. He cannot know. Not yet."

"Now go. You cannot be seen here with me. Keep a close watch on that kid. He's precious."

The next morning, Sam had not slept a wink. He still sat at his chair. As the sun rose, the forest top lit up like a jewel. The warm rays of the sun touched Sam's cheeks. It cheered him and although he was sleepy, he felt better. He knew that the day was an important one. He wanted to hide his sleeplessness from everyone. He looked into the mirror. His eyes were a little swollen and red from lack of sleep. He did some exercises to make his body feel more active, and that was it. He was fresh and ready for his second day.

It was 9 a.m. Time to go to the academy. Sam walked out of his room, met John, and together they went to the first floor to meet Mariane. Jonathan and his group were there as well, so they all took the secret passage together.

Upon arriving, they were received by their respective guides. The guides accompanied them to the chambers, where they all quietly ate their breakfast. At 10 a.m., their classes began.

All the new scholars were taken to the Forming Hall. The director of Volgarth stood there, waiting for them. "Scholars, I hope you've slept well. Your training and research start now." He paused and began again. "As you know by now, each group has one mystical science student, one medical student, and one student in the technical sciences. The perfect group comprises all three—technology, biology, and mystical science together. You will labour as if you are one, and not a group of three. Other than that, all of you will switch groups as and when instructed to. You must learn to work with new people and adapt to teams as fast as possible. The aim of your study and research here is to not only make you scholars but trained professionals, professionals who will undertake the most advanced research in any corner of this universe. I wish you all the luck for what awaits you. You will perform your research and fieldwork in groups, but classes will be held separately, depending not on your group but your area of study. While you may think that you are already experts in your field, you don't know anything about its application in the magical world. This is what you will be taught here. Now, I will request the technical science students to follow Mr Esdorg, the medical students to follow Ms Lesslie, and the mystical science students to kindly follow Kasmuji to their respective classes."

Just like the others, Sam, John and Mariane were now separated. They followed their guides in a shuffle. The classrooms were large and equipped with all modern objects. Unlike the other elements at Volgarth, all of which had more of an old-world charm to it, the classrooms epitomized modernity and technological progress. They were equipped with projectors that could project holograms into thin air, screens that had voice recognition enabled to recognize the voice of the teacher and display three-dimensional images of whatever the teacher was explaining. Automatic lights would adjust the brightness of the classroom as and when required. All the scholars looked awed by this display of technology.

As the students in Sam's class settled in, they were addressed by Kasmuji. "As the director has already mentioned, you all will be learning the application of your subjects here. By application, I mean how to use your knowledge in your field of research to tackle problems. These problems are varied, such as unlocking a mysterious door, finding a secret path, deciphering magical codes from ancient texts, and so on. You will be learning to use science to your advantage. Science has developed enough to compete with magic, and we must use it to our advantage. Let me give you an example."

Sam heard none of this. He had fallen asleep at his desk.

"Sam! Will you please come here?" Kasmuji beckoned.

His eyes still red from last night, Sam wobbled to the front of the room. Kasmuji noticed his eyes. *Maybe he is still tired from his journey,* Kasmuji thought. It could have even been the difficulty of adjusting to a new planet's atmosphere, he reasoned. So, he lay his hand kindly on

Sam's shoulders and asked, "As a mystical science student, you must have read about the Kingslace. Am I right?"

"Yes, sir," Sam promptly replied.

"So, do you know what it is?" Kasmuji asked again.

"Yes, Kingslace refers to a rope. This rope is said to be used to tie up drakons, huge mystical dragon-like creatures with four wings that can emit fire from their mouth," Sam recited.

"Drakons. Now what exactly do these things look like?" Kasmuji pointed towards the screen. A picture of a Drakon was on display.

The creature looked terrifying. Kasmuji narrated the story. "Legend has it that in ancient times, a mysterious creature appeared on Earth and began to destroy everything. No weapon could hurt the beast, no chain could tie it up. Flames from its mouth burnt down cities. Even the ocean began to evaporate from the heat of its flames. Everything was on the verge of destruction. The King of Earth then decided to take help of the magicians to save his people.

He decided to visit the Dead. For long, the earth has provided shelter to the Dead. Now, the Dead were to pay its debts. But it had also been said that one who visits them never returns. The King had already decided to sacrifice himself for his people. The King turned to his people. He told them that his forefathers had given the Dead shelter. At that time, the Dead had promised to help the Earth whenever required. They were bound by a promise. When the King demanded that the promise be kept, the Dead gave him a lace, which had so much power in it that if it was tied to the Drakon, it would destroy it. The King received the lace and the Dead made him its successor. He received all the powers of the lace. He then asked them to spare his life till he tied that lace to the Drakon and that he would return after he had destroyed the Drakon and give his life to the Dead. The Dead agreed and allowed him to remain alive till he had killed the Drakon. The brave King then went on to hunt down the Drakon. The furious battle between the

King's men and the Drakon lasted for twenty days and in the end, the King was able to tie the lace on the Drakon's leg and destroy it. But the King was greedy and did not want to part with his life. He did not return to the Dead. Soon, he turned cruel as kings do. He had the power of the lace and even the Dead could not harm him. The Dead warned the King that there would be consequences if he did not return. They waited long, expecting the King to return. But he never did. So, at an opportune moment, the Dead extracted the soul of the Drakon that had been killed by the lace and sent it back to the earth. The soul separated and formed many smaller creatures, who became dragons. The Dead thought that the dragons were enough to bring down the all-powerful King. But they had underestimated the power of the lace. The King found a way to tame the dragons using the lace and formed an army of dragons. He became invincible, and even more of a tyrant. Now, he wanted to conquer all and be the King of the Universe. That is when the asteroid hit the earth and wiped everything out. Why an asteroid, why did it hit the earth, why at that time … these are still mysteries. The lace, however, remains on earth. After the King's death, the lace was cursed. Anyone who touches it now will burn to ash. Only a Dead can touch it, but a Dead cannot be made successor to its powers. These conditions keep it safe. You all may be wondering why I have lectured on this for so long. There are powers in the universe, rulers who want to be the rulers of the entire universe. These dark powers have found a way to harness the powers of the lace. They have found the lost soul of the King. It is believed that if the soul of the King unites with the lace, an immortal evil will be born. Although these things are only written in ancient texts, we still believe them to be true. Even now, our researchers are hard at work, searching for the location of the lace before anyone else finds it."

Kasmuji pointed towards the hologram. "From carbon dating, we have been able to visualize the shape of the lace."

They all looked at the display and saw the lace, including Sam. It was about a kilometre long and shone like a diamond.

"This is what we are doing here. This is how we are trying to learn about the magical world, which our ancient texts say actually existed. Now how would you apply what you have learnt? What if you are posted to conduct research on the Kingslace? This is what we will teach you," Kasmuji explained. "It is said that the lace is under the ocean's bed. The path to it is a dangerous one. It will be your knowledge of the mystical world that will find that place, find that path, and even master the ancient magical spells that obstruct your entry through that path."

As all the students were in awe of the lace, Sam felt a different connection to it. He was not that surprised by Kasmujis story, rather he felt like he had known these things from time immemorial. As his mind fought the battle to remember the bits and pieces, he could not concentrate further on his class.

Meanwhile, in the Medical class, Ms Lesslie explained, "As medical students, your contribution to the group will be to monitor any harmful bacteria in the planets you might have to visit, structurally analyse the various creatures, provide medical assistance in case of injuries on board during a mission, or attend to the sicknesses of any crew member. The main things that will be taught to you will be knowledge about diseases mentioned in the ancient books, the biological structures of ancient creatures and so on. For example, we will now see the biological structure of a creature called the Fotles."

An image blew up on their screens.

"As you can see, a Fotles is a three-eyed horse, used by witches to travel. It has wings with a span of 200 m each. So here, you can see the structural diagram of the creature. Although these creatures that you will be studying are only alive in ancient textbooks, you are being taught about them because you and I both believe it is necessary. This is what we do. We try to find out the existence of the magical world, which our forefathers saw, whose description they jotted down in books. We believe that the universe holds more secrets than we know. We believe this because we already have evidence, and it strengthens our belief in the magical world more and more. You all will have access to those secrets as you pass your basic tests. So, this model of Fotles is based upon our studies of numerous ancient books that have been recovered from all around the universe. It has a skeletal structure …

The scene in the technical class was similar. The technical students were listening carefully to Mr Esdorg's lecture.

"Dear students, you represent the necessity of technology in the search for magic. We use technology that is available to us to enhance our search operations. Some of you will be technical engineers for spaceships; some will be controllers for robotic instruments. You will not only operate these objects but also will be responsible for the safety of your group in the field. You will be able to reach places where people can't, touch things others can't, see things. Without you, there no research is possible. Here, you will see some equipment unlike what you are used to; you will learn to operate them. You are also expected to build new equipment that could become handy in our research. Now, I am going to show you an equipment called a hemotropic neon laser glass. This laser glass enables you to see what's inside radioactive materials without even going near it. From our research so far, we have seen that most of the magical secrets are buried under materials that are highly radioactive. This glass prevents you from unnecessarily engaging with materials which can be potentially harmful. You start digging a rock that is radioactive only after you are certain of what's inside it. Now, look at the screen. The circuitry of this device …"

CHAPTER 5

My Dreams

Classes lasted the entire day. Sam, Mariane and John met for a little while at lunch, but otherwise, their schedule was very hectic. John had learnt from Kasmuji that research was increasing, new findings had enabled much progress. At the same time, AMMR had lost many researchers as it was a high-risk project. The academy was desperate for new researchers as soon as possible. And efforts were being made at Volgarth to speed up their basic training, making them ready for fieldwork as soon as possible. Thanks to this, their leisure time had been cut short.

"We won't have any time to ourselves at all. Only a lunch break during the day," John grumbled.

"I'm already so tired," added Mariane.

They finished their lunch of mushroom rice and ten different kinds of cooked meat completed by the delicious gulab jamun and kheer in desserts. As they were getting back to their classes, Sam seemed to be lost in thought.

"Are you all right Sam?" John asked him. On hearing John be so forthcoming, Mariane also added, "Yes, Sam, I have been observing you since last night. Something seems to be bothering you. Tell us, we are your friends. Maybe we can help?"

Listening to his friends and seeing their genuine concern and care for him, Sam decided to open up and trust his friends.

"I have to tell you something guys—a dream," Sam said

"What sort of dream?" Mariane asked, but they had already reached their respective classes and had no time.

Sam's entered the class, looking behind him at his friends, he loudly but calmly declared, "I will tell you guys. Tonight."

Classes ended at 4.45 p.m. All the new scholars left wearily for their respective chambers. Their tool kits were kept there. They collected all that they were expected to study from the chamber library, and then, through the secret passage, set out towards the Dorm. On the way, Sam noticed that door again. He felt as if something were calling to him from inside it, something familiar and strange at the same time. Almost like a voice calling out his name. But, with great difficulty he controlled himself. He did not want to trespass in front of everyone, he knew how strict the academy was regarding its rules and regulations. As they reached the Dorm, they headed straight to the dining hall and sat down for tea. Sam still hadn't recovered from the events of the last few days.

Soon enough, their other friends, Jane and her group joined them at the same table. At the sight of Jane, Sam soon forgot what he had been thinking. It jolted him awake. Jane really was beautiful, he thought. But because they were there, Mariane and John decided not to ask Sam about his dream, not now. They turned to a more sociable topic.

"It was exciting to learn about the Fotles. Wasn't it Mariane?" Jane chirped.

"Yes, indeed it was. I'm a medical student, and I have learnt about the anatomy of different species and their skeletal structures, but today's lecture was so different. I really enjoyed it. Oh, learning about the disease litredona was exciting." She turned to the others and explained, "It is a very dangerous disease. To be able to imagine that such a disease has a cure was amazing."

"What about you Sam? How was your day?" Jane asked.

Sam was struck by her attentive gaze. "It was good," he said, carefully. "Listening to the stories from the ancient books about many creatures, the mysteries about those creatures, the theories about locations of magical worlds—though I find it hard to believe in theories with no proof. But still, I liked the classes. Especially the one where we learnt to decipher maps, paths and that other one, where we were taught about magical spells," Sam answered.

"Oh! So you are the type of guy who needs proof for every answer. You should have been with the technical team. Why did you join mystical sciences, you will never have the proof you desire," Jane said.

"I just … followed a voice in my heart. I know that mystical science is a theoretical subject, but still I believe that magic exists. I might not have completely believed in it before, but in my two days here, I am definitely starting to believe." Sam smiled mysteriously.

Jane smiled back; his answer had not been what she had expected. As they sipped at their tea and conversation winded down, the worry he had been feeling returned. As he moved towards his room, he saw Jonathan behind him. He was whispering at him. Sam heard him say. "Don't tell anyone Sam!"

Shocked, he shouted out as Jonathan hurried towards his room. "Wait! How do you know about it? Give me an answer."

Jonathan did not stop, nor did he turn back; he entered his room and shut the door with a bang. Sam grew more confused than before. *Was he making the right decision?* He began to wonder as he opened his door and entered his dark room. *Why did he ask me not to tell anyone about the dream? What did he know?*

He muttered to himself. "I have already told my friends that I would tell them about the dream. What will I say to them now?" He paced about the room. "Wait! Why I should listen to someone who has never even smiled at me once, I should tell my friends about it."

Sam was determined to ignore Jonathan. He would tell his friends about his dream, as planned. With that Sam sat down to study, looking through his notes on deciphering and the lace and time passed by smoothly till dinner.

After dinner, Sam indicated to Mariane and John that they should come with him to the bell tower. The bell tower was an old tower, which had served as the watchtower for the Dorm before the walls had been built. From the top of the bell tower, you could see the forbidden forest on one side and the four pillars on the other. Though well maintained, the tower was now vacated. So, it was an ideal place to talk and share what you did not want anyone else to hear. They trudged up to the top of the bell tower quietly. The view was mesmerizing. Without wasting any more time, John asked, "Sam, now tell us about your dream."

Mariane too nodded. "Yes Sam, tell us."

Encouraged thus, Sam began to describe his dreams.

"I don't know what they are or why I am seeing them. After coming here, I have begun to have these strange dreams, every time I sleep. I hear strange screams. Yesterday, before tea, I fell asleep. That's when they started. Two foggy figures were near my bed. I don't know who they were. But all I heard were strange screams. They kept quiet despite my questions and led me through the path with the high walls, out of the academy and into the forbidden forest. I followed them. The forest was dark, but the two figures were shining brightly. And then there was a black shadow behind those two figures. The shadow consumed the two figures and then was everywhere … even the forest looked darker. The screams in my head grew louder and louder more painful. My head, my eyes, they felt as if they would explode"

"The next one was similar. After tea, I fell asleep. I dreamt that I was having this dream. It left me screaming and caused a huge ruckus. All the people in the dorm came out of their rooms. But no one could open the door to my room. Finally, Miss Hollande came in with Kasmuji and Mr Esdorg and they broke my door. I must have been sitting in a corner, so they took me to the bed, all the while they seemed to look at my state: my head, my eyes … but the dark shadow came again. This time, it started engulfing *all of you*. I begged it to leave my friends alone, but it kept on growing. Kasmuji was the last to go. He said something to me about secrets, but I don't exactly remember. Then the shadow came towards me and I started to suffocate in my sleep. It was then that I woke up. I was so scared I couldn't sleep the entire night."

Mariane and John looked at Sam. Their eyes were comforting and kind.

"We all have nightmares. Don't worry Sam," Mariane said.

"No, Mariane this is different. I can feel it. I'm terrified. The dreams began after Volgarth and every time I fall asleep, the same dream repeats itself. I don't know how I can sleep." Sam sighed.

"Don't worry, brother." John looked at him.

Brother!

"I will sleep with you tonight in your room. We will deal with this together," he comforted.

For the first time in his life, someone had called him "brother". His eyes welled up, He promised to himself to never let go of John. But the worry had not entirely abated. As they were talking, Mariane suddenly shrieked. Something had passed!

She shouted out. "Hey! Who is there?" A shadow rushed out from behind the door.

They all ran to the door. A man was rushing down towards the stairs. John followed as fast as he could, but the shadow man disappeared into the darkness. Crestfallen, he returned to his friends waiting at the bell tower. Sam and Mariane could not wait. They had also left the tower and were looking around, surreptitiously.

"I couldn't catch him," John apologized.

"Who would want to spy on a conversation like this, about Sam's dreams?" Mariane questioned, annoyed, and confused.

"I don't know." Sam sighed. "I don't know anything. Who would be this interested in me?"

"Sam, don't worry." Mariane patted Sam and began to lead him back to their rooms. "John and I are with you."

"I don't feel safe in this place anymore," Sam confessed.

Mariane saw how worried he was and tried to reassure him. "We will never let anyone harm you, Sam. We'll fight if we have to. Don't worry. Now let's go back to our rooms. It's late."

Saying goodbye to Mariane, John opened the door to Sam's room and they both went in. It was late and John was sleepy, so without delay John said, "Let's sleep Sam. It's late. Tomorrow we have a hectic schedule. Don't worry about the dream. I am here with you. Okay?"

John's presence was comforting to Sam and he smiled weakly. He switched off the lights lay down. They both tried to sleep. Tired from the day, John fell asleep the moment he closed his eyes. But Sam could not sleep. Fear of the dream still looming large, stalking through his mind. He pressed his eyes shut, and finally, after some time, he drowsed off to sleep.

He awoke to John's tumultuous morning rush. "Sam! Sam! Wake up! It's time for class. Don't you want to go to class today?"

John shook Sam, who slowly opened his eyes, the sleep still making him lethargic. "It's so gloomy," he argued.

"Yes, indeed. It's a cloudy day today." John was nonchalant. "The sun decided to take a break I guess."

Sam groggily sat up.

John smiled. "Okay Sam, I am going to my room to get ready for class. You get ready too. I'll see you there." Saying this, John left the room.

As soon as John left, the noises in his head began again. In a grumpy voice, someone was calling out his name.

"Sam!"

Louder, now. As if they were coming closer.

At that moment, the door to Sam's room opened slowly. It was John. He stood in front of the door, not entering. He waved his hand and gestured to Sam. Sam got up and went near him, but John back away, slowly running. Sam tried to catch up with him, but however hard he tried, he could not catch up, who seemed to be running at quite a slower pace. John went down the stairs, through the reception hall and entered the dining hall. Sam followed him.

Sam shouted, "Wait! John! Where are you going? Aren't we supposed to go to class today? Wait!"

John did not wait.

He ran to a corner of the dining hall that was behind the chair usually occupied by Miss Hollande and opened a door and went inside it. As Sam reached the door, he saw that it was pitch black inside. He could not see a thing. He hesitated. But he heard John calling. "Come on Sam. Come inside."

Tentatively, Sam decided to go in. As soon as he went inside, the door behind him shut with a bang and suddenly, everything inside lit up. Images flashes like holographic scenes. Sam could see Volgarth, his friends, his teachers, the mysterious door, the walls, the strange flowers …

Everything was flowing into one another, like someone had started a slideshow of images from his memory. The flow sped up, faster and faster. Sam could see John at a distance, still running ahead. He followed. As Sam moved through the maze of his own memories, his eyes caught the attention of the shadows he had been seeing in his dreams. He saw bright figures at first—blurry and grainy—with two human figures behind them. As he tried to look closely, the dark shadow appeared before his eyes in a flash. Sam fell backwards in shock.

The dark shadow engulfed the two figures as Sam dodged and moved ahead. Scared, he looked away, turning back to the images. He could see all the habitable, habited and formerly inhabited planets in the universe. They were all moving past him. Finally, he saw the planet Earth, his home. As he followed the trajectory of the Earth, he stumbled across something and found himself at the edge of a cliff.

John stood below that cliff. The incline was not steep, and one could climb down. As Sam started to climb down, he saw that the cliff was actually a heap, made of bones and skeletons. A huge pile of bones and skeletons. He felt awful and upset. He was stepping on them. The thought sent shivers up his spine. Reluctant to climb any further, he hesitated. And John called him again, "Hurry up Sam. We don't have all night."

"Wait," Sam stopped John. "You said it was morning. Class, remember? Now you're saying it's night! Wait!"

John did not answer and kept ahead. Sam had to put in more effort to catch up to him now; John led Sam out from the fourth pillar of Volgarth, into the wilderness outside. Sam was now very close to John. He caught hold of him from behind and as he pulled John towards himself, the surrounding suddenly changed. Sam found himself in the middle of a forest. Sam recognized it from his dreams. It was the forbidden forest.

John was now nowhere to be seen. Sam could now see the two bright figures in front of him. They had now almost taken the shape of a young man and a woman. As Sam was trying to figure out what was going on, the woman-like figure spoke, "Sam! My child. How long I have waited for this moment. Look at you!" Her voice was shaking. Her eyes were full of tears. "You have grown so big. I wish I could have been there with you ... all this time ..."

"Who are you? Do I know you? How do you know my name?" Sam asked, perplexed.

It is at this point that Sam broke. So much had passed by, but Sam seemed unmoved by those things. From the day he landed in Volgarth, he faced so many challenges, but nothing could get to his nerve. But this moment was different. The sound, the voice had a connection to his heart. His heart skipped beats when he heard the voice. There was a strange restlessness in his heart as if he had a sudden realization that he been missing something that his life was empty and hollow that he had not known love and affection. It all seemed different. It seemed like a part of him was there-right there, but he could not get to it. He could feel it, hear it, even smell it but he did not know what or who it was.

"Sam, we cannot tell you who we are now. When the time is right, you will know." They paused. "Right now, we have more important things to tell you. Remember, Sam, never give up on your dreams. The path you have chosen is the correct one. The world still does not entirely believe in magic. Even at Volgarth, everything they have on show is not magic. Some are just illusions, tricks conjured by science made to fool the students, to make them believe that the IMMR is the right path for the students to follow. But some of Volgarth is actually magic. Real magic. The very foundation of Volgarth was laid on the basis of magic. Volgarth was not made by men, only discovered by them. Much of it remains inaccessible. This universe is a treasure for those who are brave enough to set on the voyage to find the treasure. Remember Sam, if there is a treasure, there will be difficulties in procuring it, and there will be challenges—things which you have never seen, never experienced. But it is upon you to find that treasure before the dark finds it …"

Sam interrupted, "Wait! How do you know all these things and why are you telling me all this?"

"Sam, remember that you have to find the treasure." They continued without an answer, as if they were in a hurry. "Trust the people around you only after you know them well. Don't blindly trust anyone! This universe has good people and some of them will be your friends, teachers, and people you know. But the universe is comprised of worse things than you know, people who are much closer to you than you think. There is light everywhere. Only sometimes is it hidden by darkness. Always be careful and never leave your path. Work hard for what you believe, and destiny will always be with you."

The male figure now began to speak. "Sam, all these things may sound strange to you, but we know that you have the potential to find what is impossible. The universe always needs a reason to move ahead. Right now, finding the magical world is the only reason that can keep the universe moving. Everything would come to a standstill without it. Nothing will exist in this universe otherwise, Sam. You have to become the hope for your people. It's not easy. Nobody is destined to become the hope—it is only hard work that determines it. You're in Volgarth, it means that you are capable. Now, it only depends on you. We know you don't believe in magic, not really. But this is what makes you the most suitable for what lies ahead. You are a non-believer who wants to believe by finding out what lies in the unknown."

The light from the two figures began to dim. Sam could see their faces becoming blurrier and blurrier. The surrounding now became darker; fast winds were blowing through the forest, blowing away the dry leaves. Sam could see the dark shadow engulfing the two figures. It was as if a big black hole was pulling the two figures towards its infinite darkness. Sam reached out and caught onto the female figures' hand. Now he could now feel the force of the dark shadow. It was dragging her away from him. It was too much for him and he could not keep holding on, his fingers slipped, one by one.

The two figures disappeared into the darkness. The dark charm of the forest returned. So dark that for once, Sam felt that he was inside the shadow itself. Then he saw John again. John stood at some distance away from Sam. *So he was in the forest*, he reasoned.

At that moment, the shadow was again in front of Sam. It moved past him, falling deeper into the forest. Sam decided to follow it. The forest grew denser and darker as Sam moved forward, trailing the shadow. He had decided to not let go. It led Sam to the other side of the forest, the end of it. Sam could not believe his eyes.

What stood before him was drastically different in comparison to the forest he knew. One side of it seemed dark and frightening, while the other side was beautiful and full of life and light. There were rivers, trees bearing fruits and ample light, which only amplified the beauty of the place. There were mountains and waterfalls in the distance, and there were animals, horses that could fly and resembled the Fotles, birds that sang and fishes in the river. It was a whole new world.

As Sam moved around looking astonished, the place gradually became darker, as if the light from the place was being sucked away. In a matter of moments, the entire place was black, exactly like the forbidden forests. The dark shadow could no longer be seen. The glamour had faded, and Sam suddenly realized where he was. He did not know the way out. He started to back away from where he stood. The tall trees with gnarled branches left a path that looked scary and puzzling. The mist of the night blocked out even the tiniest fragment of moonlight entering the forest. He was lost.

As he wandered anxiously, he saw a light, very dim and small, flickering in the distance. Sam saw it as one sees hope. It was possible that the figures had been speaking of this moment. He reasoned that his direction was correct, and despite the darkness and obstructions in his path, light would always be shining beyond it. He would have to work harder to achieve what lay beyond it. As he approached the light, he saw John waiting for him there.

"I have been waiting for you, Sam. Let's go now," he said.

Sam knew that he was out of the forbidden forest. He followed John and they went back down the same path through which they had come. On reaching the fourth pillar of Volgarth, Sam suddenly realized that a huge pile of human bones and skulls were inside that pillar. He hesitated at first, but on seeing John, his fear abated, and he began to follow him. However, this time, there was no pile of skulls and bones. Instead, a staircase rose up. They began their climb.

"Come this way, Sam. We are about to reach the Dorm." John said as he led the way.

Sam followed him up the spiral staircase. As John turned a corner, Sam lost sight of him. Sam began to climb quicker, two steps at a time. But his eyes were not focused on the ground and as he took his next step up the stairs, he fell through, down through a steep incline. The drop never came, the hole seemed infinite. As Sam fell, a strange feeling overcame him. He started to feel numb. It felt as if the darkness had finally taken him in its grab and he was being consumed by it. He wasn't sure whether he would live or die once he hit the ground. He kept falling and the end was nowhere near. He shut his eyes and could only see darkness. He was terrified and scared. He wanted to shout for help but could not move his lips. His body felt paralyzed and cold.

Suddenly, the voice of the two figures struck him, "Sam, remember! There is light everywhere. Only sometimes it is hidden by the darkness. You just have to look beyond."

Sam opened his eyes in a flash and tried to as closely as he could; he wanted to ascertain what was below. And in that instant, a bright flash of light appeared, and he was drawn towards it. The darkness was replaced by light and it shone brighter than anything Sam had ever seen. He disappeared into the light …

"Sam! Sam! Wake up, buddy. Its morning. Look how bright the day looks today." John was shaking Sam, trying to wake him up.

John could feel how cold Sam's body was as he held him. Sam slowly opened his eyes. The last thing he remembered was falling off the cliff and entering the light. John said, "Hey Sam! Why is your body so cold? You slept for a long time. Don't you want to go to class today? Wake up and get ready. The sun is shining."

Sam could not determine what was going on. He could make up his mind as to whether it was a reality or a dream. Was the fall a dream, or was it the morning? Which John was the dream and which the real? His head was aching. But he woke up and looked outside. It really was a bright day. He saw John standing in front of him. Nothing was blurry now. John was smiling at him.

"So, Sam, did dream last night? I slept great—the best sleep of my life."

Sam didn't know how to respond. This was real, he had decided. The other John had been a dream.

But even if it was just a dream, it had shaken him up. There were more questions than before. He did not where to start or why. John clapped him on his back suddenly. He asked, "Hey! Sam. Where are you lost? You had a bad dream again?"

Sam sighed. "Yes. This one was different from the others. I'm confused. It was disturbing. Remember the two figures I told you about? I saw their faces. It felt like I was connected to them in some way, but I don't know how. They told me … a lot of things. I also saw you. You led me towards them into the forbidden forests and also brought me back. I also saw the shadow and a whole new side to the forbidden forest, full of light and life and mysterious creatures."

John started to laugh, "Ha! Sam. What did you say?"

"I was there? You probably saw me because I was sleeping here. I can't be related to your dreams anyway. But Sam, I must say, your dreams are becoming really interesting. I guess there is something fishy about them. You should talk to someone in the academy, Sam. You also mentioned faces. Who were they, do you know them? Did they have names?"

"No, I have never seen them before. I don't know. They said I would know when the time comes." Sam sighed again. "You are right. I must discuss it with someone. I think Kasmuji will be best."

"Yeah. He's our guide, after all. Now get ready for class. I will see you there." John went out of Sam's room and closed the door behind him.

Sam pulled off his covers and decided to forget things for a while. He had class. In any case, he would discuss the matter with Kasmuji …

CHAPTER 6

The Battle of Arksoles

The students reached Volgarth in the morning. They moved in their groups towards their respective classes according to their schedule, but they were told that the batch would be taught together. After which, they could move to their respective departmental labs for practical exercises. They would be taught the history of the magical world.

The class was supposed to be taken by Mr Gregor, a new teacher. The students were led to the conference room, which was the biggest class in Volgarth. As the students settled in, they were joined by Mr Gregor.

"Good Morning, students, I am Gregor Raichardson. I am your history teacher. In this class, you will be taught a manuscript. This manuscript contains information about the history of humanity and the wars of the universe. When we found this manuscript, it inspired us to think about the various beliefs persistent in different parts of the universe about magical worlds. Basically, you will be learning about the past, what we believe happened in the past, how the idea of the existence of a magical world came into being."

Mr Gregor continued as he sneezed and wiped his nose. It appeared as if he had caught an instance of cold.

"It is said that many million years ago, when humanity was only counted among a small population of the total life forms in this universe, humans inhabited only a few select planets. During this time, humanity stumbled upon the magical world. They realized that they were not the only species living in the universe. There were species more superior than them. The manuscript records the presence of a Creator, who, knowing the potential of humans, created species superior to humans. The Creator blessed them with powers to maintain the precarious balance of the universe. At the time, humanity did not understand these powers. Humans claimed they were supernatural and began to worship them. Humanity's first encounter with such a creature began with the Lomder, a three-headed wolf. The wolf was said to bring rain where he went. During droughts especially, humans began to worship this wolf. They began to offer him smaller animals as sacrifice and tribute. This was the first. As time passed, more and more creatures came into contact with humanity, and people kept worshipping them. After many ages of supernatural belief, humans encountered a species that looked almost similar to them. This species had powers and could control the mysterious creatures. Humans then perceived these species to be their Gods and began to worship them instead; the creatures were then represented as their vehicles of faith. This species is known as the ancient species of Arksoles. This powerful species taught humanity the art of writing, painting, agriculture, building, making tools and more. Human, under the shadow of this superior species, began to develop and grow at a rate even the Creators had not expected. Some wanted the power of the Arksoles and worship them with such an intent, but the Arksole knew that humans were a newer species and that giving them powers would have serious repercussions. They instead offered their infrastructural help. They built huge structures: dams, provided humans with electricity, weapons to hunt, taught them the art of cooking, taught them about metals, their uses, the use of fossil fuels and machinery. But the Arksoles are a race like any other, and some were power-hungry, while others were not. Humans were able to discern that the Arksoles, too, wanted to become the rulers of the universe. Among the humans, some were similar. They wanted to rule. The Arsksoles leading such a coup, allied with some of the humans, and blessed them with evil powers. These humans were called witches. They provided the witches with power on the condition that when they would set sail to conquer the universe, the witches had to travel with them. The witches were permitted to become the rulers of the planets where there would be human species. The witches set out."

Mr Gregor wiped his nose again.

"All the weapons and metals of the humans were no match for the witches. They began to conquer humans. One planet at a time. They captured those who opposed them and tortured them. As it does, it led to chaos everywhere. The other Arksoles washed their hands off this mess. Instead, they gave their worshippers powers and called them the Knights of Arksoles. A war ensued between the two powers, the witches, and the Knights of Arksoles. Magic was used as a weapon both, in the battlefield and off it. The war was so vast that its ripples were felt throughout the farthest corners of the universe. Humans, a relatively new species, had been dragged into this war. The outcomes were devastating, and scores of lives were lost. The war could be called egotistic, if you ask me. The Arksoles could have stopped it if they wanted to but neither wanted to call defeat. The war had turned dirty and base, good and bad could no longer be determined. It had now become a fight between two of the same, one Arksoles group or another. Power was granted as time passed. Humans were most affected during the course of this war. It had destroyed their homes, their source of sustenance; the future of humanity was at risk. The witches and the knights would not stop. Their own people were dying, there was suffering everywhere, food was scarce and epidemics spread like wildfires. The human population was greatly reduced across the universe. The species which had the potential to become the strongest of them all was now at the verge of extinction. It was at that time that a brave and valiant knight, Sorceon, decided to appeal to the Creators to stop this war. He set sail for the most difficult journey that the universe had to offer—to find the Creators and ask for their help. The Arksoles learnt of it and were afraid. If he succeeded, it would mean the end of their powers. Not long ago, the Arksoles had been a similar race, just like humans. One of them had been able to complete a similar journey to reach the Creators. The Creators had blessed him and had asked him to join their gathering, but he had instead asked for the powers to be distributed among his race, the Arksoles. The powers came as a blessing for the Arksoles. They were in the midst of a famine, but with their powers, they could now travel to other planets. By colonizing these planets, they could procure food and shelter both. They became the most superior species. Now, if

Sorceon could complete this journey as well, humans would be blessed with similar powers or powers of a greater degree. The Arksoles would no longer hold their position among humans. They had to stop him. They summoned the most powerful witches and asked them to stop Sorceron. Sorceron's journey was to begin on the thirteenth day of the moon year, and he was alone. Moreover, all the other remaining knights were required to stop the witches. Sorceron, however, was accompanied by a werewolf called Ricean. Ricean was the most powerful werewolf alive at the time. The knights designed a spacecraft with their powers and Sorceron and Ricean set sail on their voyage to find the Creators. They ascertained where to go with the help of an ancient manuscript that was believed to have been written in the aftermath of creation. It contained faint hints regarding the location but the language in which it was written was very ancient and no one knew to read it."

At this point, Mr Gregor paused to take a breath.

"First, Sorceron had to find someone who could interpret the manuscript. He had never been on such a voyage. Before he began his journey, Sorceron was met by an old raven at his house which said that it could read some images of the manuscript. Of the images it could read, all of them conveyed danger, it seemed to ward Sorceron off. The Creators had filled the path leading to them with dangerous creatures and vicious traps and even the bravest could not cross them. No one knew how to overcome those challenges. The act required Soceron to be brave and strong, and to have the brains to be able to reach his destination. Sorceron and Ricean set out into the vast universe on their spaceship. It is said that the spaceship was so powerful that it could move at a speed twice that of light. Its trail could be seen from miles away, thus the witches found it easier to trace them. The witches knew that the spacecraft was faster than them and they could not catch it, at least not in space. However, they knew that the spacecraft needed to make a stop, every thirty days, as it produced an enormous amount of heat that could melt away the surface of the spacecraft. The passengers too needed to rest to avoid the strain on their bodies. The witches decided that they would stop them when they made a stop, killing them if necessary. During the first thirty days of their voyage, Sorceron and Ricean wandered around the vast universe, trying to find a way through the riddles. They went from planet to planet, star to star, they searched every asteroid, every star belt, rock belt they encountered, but they could not find any leads. They knew that they were nowhere near their destination and they had little time. The war was growing bloodier and the suffering only increased. The Knights were losing ground and it was becoming more difficult to defend themselves. They encountered many species, but none were intelligent enough to tell them about the path. Finally, after thirty tedious days of travel and lots of disappointment, they decided to haul in for their first stop."

Mr Gregor had to pause again, as he sneezed and wiped his nose. "Sorry," he mumbled and continued.

"They stopped at a planet known as Emphor. As you know, Emphor is a beautiful planet and is home to a species called the Resgords. Resgords are one of the first species to have arrived in the universe. They were considered among the most ancient species. Although they were not as intelligent as humans, over time they had developed their own written and spoken language. Resgords lived for many years, accumulating knowledge. An elderly Resgord was as intelligent as a thousand humans. They were said to be the first species created and most of the ancient manuscripts were written by them. This included the one Sorceron was carrying. Since Resgords were the first species to be created, they were believed to be located closer to the Creators. In earlier ages, the Resgord elders could directly visit the Creators and discuss matters of importance. The Creators, too, relied on them. Some conspiracies and a war later, the Creators cursed the Resgords for their interference. To restore balance, all the elderly Resgords were stripped of their long lives and killed. The Creators now saw them as a threat and ordered that all Resgords be killed. However, they were also reluctant to kill their firstborn, and instead, they displaced them, allowing the Resgords to live on a planet called Emphor—far away and isolated from any other creation. They were stripped of their benefits and were cursed—no Resgord could ever visit or come in contact with the Creators; if any Resgord even attempted to reach the Creators, he or she would be burnt to ashes immediately. The Resgords were also stripped of their manuscripts and parts of their memories before being sent off to Emphor. The Resgords were since known to have been extinct. Even the most powerful Arksoles had no idea about their existence. When Sorceron landed on Emphor, he did not know the name of the planet or who inhabited it. His first impression was that the planet was uninhabited but otherwise full of beauty and sustenance. There were water and trees with fruits—it looked like a perfect planet to house life. Sorceron was shocked to find no sign of it, except for the trees and plants. Even its waters had no creatures swimming in it. Ricean and he decided to set up their camp near a waterfall and rest for some time. They ate food and they took rest. In his memoirs, Sorceron records these moments. He wrote the following lines …"

Another sneeze interrupted Mr Gregor's words. "I think the cold has finally gotten the better of me. Anyway, let us continue with the memoir. How contrasting is this universe! On one side, such a grim war is being fought, and here it's so peaceful. Who would say that so much blood is being split somewhere else within the same universe." Mr Gregor trailed off and stopped. He looked at his students, most of whom were listening in rapt attention. "Well, let's take a break now. Or else I will find you all asleep. We'll stop for fifteen minutes and return to the class after that. I can see some of you at the back already nodding off."

But most of the students were in no mood to leave the class or for the story to stop. They all grumbled and sighed. Sam spoke up. "Sir, can't we take a break after we finish the story? None of us is in a mood to leave it there and take a break. I'm eager to know what happened next. Please, sir, complete the story." The other students supported Sam.

Mr Gregor smiled and said, "Ah, Sam. I know. This is an interesting story. Every batch reacts the same way. They don't want to leave the class without hearing the end. But, even if you don't need a break, I do. So please, have patience." Saying this, Mr Gregor left his chair and trudged out of the class.

The students filed out after him, washing their faces and straightening their uniforms. They returned hastily. They were all consumed by thoughts about the war—the war that changed humanity and life in this universe. What would happen on Emphor, would Sorceron find the Creators, what would happen to the Arksoles and the witches and the knights. They were so lost in their individual thoughts about the war that they did not even talk to each other.

When Mr Gregor arrived, he was surprised to see all the students sitting quietly in their seats. They were all lost somewhere. He entered the hall, clicked his fingers and said, "Students, I am here now. Exit your dreams, everyone. We have an interesting story ahead of us. So, where were we?"

Jane replied, "Sir, you were reading from Sorceron's memoirs that he was wondering about the peace in Emphor and the war on the other side of the universe."

Mr Gregor responded immediately, "Yes."

With the narrative beginning again, the students settled into their seats, excited.

Mr Gregor continued, "Sorceron and Ricean fell asleep near the waterfall. However, the Resgords had already sensed that an unidentified spacecraft had landed on their home planet. It had been ages since another species had landed on Emphor. They knew that none knew about their presence since the war and they sensed a danger unlike any other. So, they sent out their best hunters to hunt down the spacecraft and bring any living creature on board to the elders. Over the ages, the Resgords had developed a defensive shield for themselves, to protect themselves. If any space traveller were to stumble upon their planet, they would first see that the planet as uninhabited. Once discovered, the planet cannot be discovered again by the same travellers." The Creators were in on this ruse They too had made sure that the path to Emphor was not recognizable again. Also, the Resgords were instructed to capture the travellers, if any. Ordinary space travellers who had come to their planet by chance or accident were let go. But their memory in Emphor had to be wiped. Although they never had to implement this instruction as no one had ever found them, they were prepared. At evening the hunters finally reached the spacecraft. They were astonished to see how advanced it looked. The Resgords could remember some similar during the war and days of glory. A hunter found Sorceron and Ricean, lying near the waterfall. As soon as he saw them, he called the others and they went towards Sorceron and Ricean. They circled around them and crept closer and closer. Sorceron writes that the light was dim there and that there were forest bugs, so we may imagine them at the scene. As Sorceron opened his eyes, he saw a strange-looking species standing in front of him, looking down at him. They were somewhat like human beings but had longer ears and bigger eyes and a round face with thin lips—scary, right?"

Mr Gregor laughed.

"Certainly, Sorceron jumped in alarm and Ricean reacted to it and woke. As soon as they both stood up, the hunters attacked them and made an effort to pin them down. Ricean, the werewolf, started to growl to warn the hunters. The hunters were speaking a language that Sorceron and Ricean could not understand. But Sorceron and Ricean had believed the planet to be uninhabited! As they stood, waiting to defend themselves against an attack, one of the hunters used an arrow blower and small arrows struck both of them in the neck. As soon as the arrows struck their neck, they knew. Their heads began to feel heavy and they fell to the ground as their eyes closed. When they awoke, and Sorceron mentions this, they found themselves surrounded by older versions of the same creatures. Their heads still felt heavy due to the poison in the arrows. Their vision was still blurry. As they tried to get up, they found themselves tied. Sorceron then spoke up, he says. He asked, 'Who are you? Why have you captured us? Why have you tied us up?' There was complete silence. The Resgords did not speak a word but were staring at them. Sorceron asked again, 'Please tell us who you are and what you want from us. Speak. You cannot capture us like this without a reason for it.' And they heard a voice from distance, 'You will tell us who you are and what is your purpose is here. You have come to our home and so we will not reply to your questions. You are bound to reply to ours.'" The oldest of them had spoken. He was very wrinkled and wore a white robe, his hair was grey and so were his eyebrows. He walked with the help of a stick and slowly. He came near them and asked again, 'Tell us who you are and what your purpose is. How did you find us?' Sorceron replied, 'We don't know anything about this planet. We did not even know that this planet was inhabited when we first arrived here. We're as shocked as you, we haven't heard your name where we come from, or even what your species are called! We are just space travellers who have stumbled upon this planet. We had to land here because our spacecraft needed to rest. It's been thirty days since we have begun travelling, and due to the supra-sonic speed of our spacecraft, we have to! According to the universal laws, you cannot keep a space traveller who has stumbled upon your planet captive.' Don't teach us the universal laws. We know them better than you do. But since you claim to be space travellers, tell us your purpose of travel and what you seek?' The old Resgord asked. 'We can't tell you about our purpose. It's prohibited for us to discuss it with any strangers. We cannot trust you.' Sorceron said. 'Well, in that case, we are afraid we cannot let you go. A space traveller with a hidden motive can be considered an enemy—according to universal laws. So unless you agree to tell us what you're looking for, you will be made prisoner here.'"

Mr Gregor paused to catch his breath and continued.

"The old man directed the hunters to take both of them away. As they were being grabbed and hauled away to the prison, Sorceron tried to figure out how to get out of this situation. He knew that their going to prison would mean the end of the human race and glory for the witches. Time was already precious and now even that little time was being taken away from them. During that moment an idea struck Sorceron. He decided to show his captors the manuscript he had with him. He remembered being told that only the most ancient and unseen species could read the manuscript. Although the origin of that species was thought to be extinct, there were rumours that a handful of them still survived in an unreachable planet. He considered the probability that his captors were none other than the long-lost Resgords. So, he decided to listen to his gut and called out, 'Wait! I have something to show you all. If you can recognize the object, we can tell you our purpose.' 'But why should we allow you to show us anything. You have come to our planet and now you are our prisoners, so why should we trust you. It may as well be a trick to fool us and run away,' the old Resgord said. 'You must allow us to show it to you. I believe it is something that belongs to all of you. Please trust us and let us bring it out. I have to say, according to the laws, we are allowed to defend ourselves as free space travellers, even if we have been imprisoned,' Sorceron insisted.

The students were hanging on to every word. Mr Gregor cleared his throat—somewhat for dramatic effect—and carried on. "After much discussions and pleading, the elders finally decided to give them a chance and agreed to at least look at what Sorceron was talking about. 'Okay, show us what you have. But remember, if it is a trick, you will be killed,' the old Resgord said. Sorceron took the manuscript out of his robe, unfolded it and held it out to the elders. The elders could not believe their eyes. It was a manuscript written by their ancestors, one of the oldest ones. It had been ages that they had seen something so old. The younger Resgords hadn't even known of its existence. It brought tears to the elders' eyes, overwhelmed on seeing their ancient manuscripts, recalling the war and the curse and long-forgotten memories. The old Resgord came forward, smiling at Sorceron and asked, 'Where did you get this? What purpose does it serve to you?' And Sorceron said, calmer than ever, 'Are you the Resgords? Is this manuscript written by your ancestors? Please tell us what you know about this manuscript and what is written in it.' As the old Resgord was about to pick up the manuscript and gauge it, he was pulled back by the other elders. A vivacious discussion in their language ensued. Sorceron could not understand what was going on. He could not go near them as they were still tied up. After some time, the old Resgord came to him and said, 'We are grateful to you for having brought this to us and to for showing it to us. This is one of the first-ever written records made in this universe. But we cannot share any information regarding this manuscript unless we know your purpose. We will only try to interpret the manuscript if your purpose is worthy of our attention, and if by any means we find your purpose to be evil and unworthy, you will either be imprisoned for life or killed immediately. So, you have no other option. Tell us your purpose or face the consequences.' Sorceron understood. They were stuck. Ricean interrupted and whispered into Sorceron's ears, 'Is it safe for us to tell them the truth? What if they were sent by the Arksoles? What if they don't want us to meet the Creators?' Sorceron comforted Ricean, and in the process, convinced himself. He told him, 'I think it is safe for us to tell them the truth. They said that they recognize the manuscript and can interpret it. We both know that we need help to interpret it. Also, if they had been sent by the Arksoles, they would have killed us by now. They already have the manuscript and they cannot get any more information out of us anyway; they know that we cannot interpret it alone.' Ricean agreed and decided to tell them everything. And so they did."

Mr Gregor let out a deep breath. "Sorceron writes that it took a long while to explain their situation—the war, the birth of humans, the Arksoles, the finding of supernatural creatures, their worshipping, the arrival of Arksoles, the good and the bad Arksoles, their power-hungry grabs, the powers of the Arksoles, the birth of the witches, their merciless use of power to rule the human race, the need of the Arksoles to create the Knights of the Arksole, the war between the witches and the knights, how the war had become a competition of power now. And mostly, he recounted the loss of lives, hunger, starvation, the sufferings of the human race, and the desperate need to save humanity. Sorceron told them of his own identity. 'I am Sorceron and I am a Knight of the Arksoles.' After this, Sorceron said, 'This is why it was decided that I should travel across the universe and find the Creators as soon as possible. No other Knight could accompany me as we were already outnumbered and needed as many knights as possible to protect our people from the witches to remain on Earth. Ricean here is a species called the werewolf. They are like humans but have the blood of a wolf and can transform into one whenever. The fate of humankind rests on us both now. The only clue we have that leads to the path of the Creators is this manuscript. We know that it was written by Resgords and that this manuscript has something, something that will lead us to that path. We are desperate. Please help us. We don't have much time. Our people need us.' They discussed this among themselves, and finally, the old Resgord came up to them and said, 'We elders understand how you must be feeling. Long ago, some of us were involved in a similar war to protect our race. We were the first intelligent species to be created by the Creators, meant to become the most superior species in the universe. We are not born intelligent but acquire intelligence through experience because of our long-life span. Being the most intelligent species at that time and also the first, we enjoyed certain privileges from the Creators. Our elders could meet them directly and we also advised the Creators in the early days of the universe. But, with intelligence comes greed, some of our elders saw the potential to rule this vast universe. Some of our firstborn elders had become intelligent and daring enough to challenge the Creators. In their greed, they forgot that they could not emerge victorious against the ones who created them. The result of this interference would only be loss. They failed to understand what consequences the war with the Creators would have on our race. They went on to fight the Creators in order to defeat them and become rulers of the universe. They had even forced the others, my friends and family, to join them in war and those who resisted were killed. I was part of that war, I saw my own people die, saw the scarcity of food and water, the suffering, all that blood. But the elders were finally defeated and captured, then killed for their interference. The Creators knew that our intelligence had no limits and that the survival of any one of us could destroy everything precious. So, as a punishment brought upon us by our elders—they recommended a genocide."

Mr Gregor's face was grim now.

"But the Creators pitied us. So many of us were innocent and had been forced into this war … after all, we were their firstborn. Without risking the consequences of allowing us to live with the other species, they decided to send us to this planet—Emphor. We were told that we could live freely here and continue to prosper, but we could never leave this planet. They made sure no one could come, either. We are located in the most secret and unknown portion of this universe, the path to which was made like a maze so none could easily find it. If someone did, we were told to let them go only after wiping their memories of this place and the path leading to this place. You are our first traveller, and we couldn't take the risk. We may have been harsh, but were only fighting against what we believed could be our downfall. The Creators sent us here and took away all our manuscripts, anything that could give us more intelligence than we needed. They wanted to make sure that none would access the knowledge our elders had. Until now, we had believed that they had destroyed the manuscripts. You have found the first manuscript written by our race! The language is very old. Over time, our language has changed, but we believe we can still interpret it. But remember, we were cursed by the Creators, we can never meet them again. If we even attempt to we would be immediately burned to ashes. After saying this, the old Resgord was called in by the other elders and they again began discussing something. After a while, the old Resgord returned and said, 'We elders have decided. We shall interpret the manuscript. Your cause has been deemed noble, and we empathize with your pain. But we must warn you, it is the most dangerous path in this universe. Even the bravest fear to attain what you seek. The Creators still keep an eye on us. So, even if they have prohibited us from meeting them, they have left open a channel that only goes one way—theirs. The channel is part of the old one used by our ancestors to reach the Creators. This manuscript most probably contains information about this channel, which may be the only way to reach your destination. There may be some other paths that lead to the Creator but only the Creators know them. But for us, this is the only path. It is a one-way channel. If you are just and your heart is pure, then you will find a direction upon entering the channel. Remember! whichever direction you find, you have to travel opposite to it. The direction you will find will contain all that you wish for. It will heal all your deepest wounds and will give you everything that you have lost, all your sorrows will go away if you take this direction, but it is not the path to the Creator. This is the hardest part, to resist everything and take the opposite direction. Besides this, many supernatural forces await you. But, as the channel for we used ran both way, it makes it easier to know all we can about this channel. It might reduce the time you spend travelling considerably.'"

Mr Gregor smiled and let the students absorb everything. Then, he spoke again.

"Sorceron and Ricean saw hope. Not for themselves, but for the entire human race. After thirty days spent tireless scouring the universe, they were in the right place. Although finding the Resgords had been a coincidence, they knew that they were in the right place and among the right people. They saw this as ordained by the Creators themselves, who must have wanted them to save humanity. That the Resgord elders could interpret the manuscript came as a relief, but they still were nervous. They hoped that the manuscript could be read, despite being an older dialect and still interpreted. At this point, Ricean could not help but wonder how could the old Resgord speak their language. He was the only one among the Resgords who could speak it. It was night now, and the old Resgord approached Sorceron and Ricean and asked them to spend the night with them in their huts, assuring them that the elders would work through the night to try and interpret the manuscript. They could then begin their journey the next day. He said, 'You both must have some food and get some sleep. If your journey is to begin tomorrow, you may not get much rest. You will need all your energy to reach them.' Seeing the opportunity, Ricean, at this moment, asked the old Resgord, "None of the other Resgords know our language. But you do—you are the only Resgord here to know our language. May I know how that has come to be?" The old Resgord replied, "When I was younger, long before the war, the Creators were deciding the letters of the language you speak. My father was among the elders there; he was one of the elders to have advised them on this matter. When he would come home, he would teach it to me.' There was a faint smile on the face of the old Resgord. He continued, 'I would always ask him why I needed to learn this funny language, and he would always pat me on my back and say that the language was for a future species, one that would be the most superior and most beautiful creation of the Creators. He said that I would be able to interact with this superior species and bring about the mutual growth of both our species and theirs, that I would be able to bring the two most superior species of this universe together, that I might need to help when the time comes. I suppose you may say that, now, I feel that he knew what was to pass, all those years ago.' There were traces of tears down his cheeks. 'Now, you both come with me. Eat. The elders have organized a feast for you—you have given us our first manuscript, a token from our days of glory.' As they were heading towards the feast, Sorceron asked the old Resgord, 'Do you have a name?' The old Resgord smiled and replied, 'Yes, my name is Schehil.' Sorceron and Ricean both followed the old Resgord to the feast. It was a grand feast set under the open skies of Emphor. A large pyramid of fire was the centre stage of the feast. All the important Resgords and their families attended the feast. There was dance and there was music that could be heard from miles away. As the woman danced and the children played, the air was filled with the fragrance of the food. They had different types of meat; riflo, which was a unique bread; rice; different types of soup; vegetables; and sweets that Sorceron and Ricean had seen for the first time. Sorceron and Ricean along with all the Resgords feasted and enjoyed. After they had eaten their fill, Sorceron and Ricean were taken to a hut to sleep. As they lay there, Schehil returned, 'The elders are going to try and interpret the manuscript tonight. They are going to perform a secret ceremony and ask for the help of our ancestors. Remember, whatever happens, do not go out of this hut at night at any cost! It is strictly prohibited for an outsider to witness this ceremony, or even be present in our huts when it is being performed. Only the elders are allowed. Not even the younger Resgords may see this ceremony. Therefore, we have specially marked your hut. But, do not worry. We will do whatever we can to help you. Now, have a good night's sleep.' In the darkness of the night, the elders waited for everyone to fall asleep. They began their work. The secret ceremony of Siklau began, the first time after the war. They believed that the Creators would not be enraged by this as they were only helping the human race survive. They even hoped, that on seeing this, the Creators would allow their race to return to the open universe, no longer hiding, able to live with the other species in the many planets of the universe."

There was pin-drop silence in the room.

"Siklau was performed to summon the soul of their ancestors and seek advice and help from them. The ceremony took all night and, the Resgords and the summoned ancestors worked tirelessly to decipher the manuscript and save the human race. All night, Sorceron and Ricean were woken by strange sounds. They understood nothing of what was going on, and the sounds scared them. But they remembered Schehil's words and forced themselves to sleep each time they woke. The next morning, Sorceron and Ricean were approached by the elders. Schehil spoke, 'What we are about to tell you is among the biggest secrets kept by this universe. We were able to interpret the manuscript ... we do not know what consequences this shall have on us if we tell you what we found out. We were even questioned by our ancestors, who asked us whether this was worth it. But we had decided. We shall tell you everything. The manuscript was written in the form of riddles. As you thought, it has a description of the path leading to the Creators. We cannot tell you the meaning of the riddles, as it is you who must decipher it. We have only translated the manuscript to your language. The two most important riddles in the manuscript tell us about the path. The first of them is: Where the light meets the dark, where the universe bends its way, where there is no escaping the truth, where there is no power neither stands, where time meets space—there lies the heart of the bravest, beating by the power of the one who created it. And the second riddle goes: At the end, there will be no end. The heart will beat fast and the mind will stop its thinking. It will be a test of trust. Leap into the darkness, only then will you find light. The light will show you your end, and the dark will show you life, but only you can choose. Besides these confounding words, the manuscript also mentions the forces of gravity. It will affect your bodies and lead to dizziness, hallucinations, headaches. Several powerful creatures will obstruct your path. You have to travel through darkness to get to the light. The paths will test your strength, senses, intelligence, bravery, patience, and your heart—your strength of character. We hope that you reach the Creators and save your species. We will provide you with food and water to help you during your journey.' At that moment, a Resgord elder came running towards Schehil; concern could be seen on his face. He began to shout at Schehil in their language. All the Resgords nearby who heard began to panic. They murmured among one another. Schehil came to Sorceron, saying, 'We are doomed because of you. Why have you come to our planet—Oh, why did we believe in you and help you? See what you have brought upon us. Oh, we should have known.' Sorceron and Ricean were shocked by these words. They could already see that chaos had ensued. They questioned, 'What has happened? Have we done something we should not have? We followed all your instructions. We didn't even step out from our beds! Please, tell us what has happened.' Schehil replied in a shaky voice, 'It's the manuscript you have brought to us. It was cursed. We didn't know. The Creators had put a curse on the manuscript. The manuscript had other words written on it—hidden beneath the first. Those words were not visible until this morning. Even the souls of our ancestors could not discern the presence of the curse.' Ricean interrupted, 'What were those words? What is the curse?' Schehil replied in a voice full of terror, 'It had our doom written on it. It was written that the manuscript would curse the writers, the Resgords, if they were to try and attain any knowledge of what had once existed. The entire race is cursed with destruction. Even those who have created this life cannot stop it.'

Even Mr Gregor was now wrapped up in this story that he himself was telling.

"Sorceron and Ricean were dumbstruck on hearing this. They did not know what to do or how to save the Resgords from what was to come. As they rushed around in a panic, they saw bright small spacecraft falling from the sky. They were numerous and it looked as if the sky was filled with fireflies. Schehil held Sorceron by his robe; shook him and said, 'Doomsday is here. You have brought this upon us. We cannot escape this time.' Sorceron said, 'Please do not blame us. How could we have known that the manuscript would cause this? Had we known, we would have never asked you to interpret it. Please don't worry, if we have brought this upon you, we will save you.' Schehil understood that Sorceron and Ricean were going to perish, just as they were and decided to take them to where the rest of them had gathered. The other elders and youth of the Resgord community opposed this. They protested that Sorceron and Ricean not be let in. According to them, the outsiders—demons, they were now called—were responsible for their misery. But Schehil convinced the elders, and although not all of them agreed, Sorceron and Ricean were allowed to go with them to the sacred temple, their hiding place. As the Resgords ran towards their temple, located 100 feet below the ground, their last resort, they hoped that they would not be noticed underneath the ground as the temple was perfectly camouflaged. After they had all entered, the doors were sealed and everyone sat nervously praying and pleading. Meanwhile, Sorceron wondered who had attacked Emphor. He felt as if he could recognize the space ships, he had seen them before. Soon, from within the temple, they heard the humming of spacecraft searching the planet. After some time, they heard a voice boom, "We are the Witches of Arksoles. We have come here to kill Sorceron and Ricean. We know they are here, hiding. We command the inhabitants of this planet to surrender them to us. If you do not give them to us, we will destroy your planet and kill every living thing on it. Wherever you are hiding, we will find you. If we cannot find you, we will make sure that this planet vanishes from the universe. We turn it to ash … but if you give them to us, we will spare your race."

Some of the students drew a sharp breath in anticipation, making Mr Gregor pause briefly.

"The room was silent. All the Resgords began to stare at Sorceron and Ricean. Sorceron began to speak, "I know what you are thinking. Don't worry, we will surrender. If this is the only way to save all of you, we will do it ourselves. But we know the witches, have sparred with him. Even if they have said that they will spare you, we don't they will keep their word. First, they will kill us, and then kill all of you, destroy the planet and leave ash behind. This is what they always do. Schehil suddenly spoke, 'I don't understand how the witches have come here with such a large force—if the exact route is not known to any, no spacecraft should be able to reach Emphor. How did they get to this place? The Creators have made sure that this would never happen, someone must have guided them here—but who? You are the only travellers to have ever reached and it does not seem possible that you yourself have guided them to kill you. So how have they arrived in such large numbers?' Sorceron and Ricean considered his question. Sorceron quickly found the answer and said, 'They must have followed the light from the boosters of our spacecraft. Since our spacecraft can move at supra-sonic speeds, it produces a very bright light that can be seen from miles away in space. The light travels, and after being reflected by the spacecraft, it goes a particular distance. As we moved, the light must have left a trail. We knew that the other party of Arksoles had sent an army of witches behind us, but their spacecraft were small and could not catch up to us. They must have decided to wait until we stopped at a planet where they could attack and kill us.' The Resgords who had already been protesting against helping Sorceron and Ricean were now even more furious. They started to blame them and as they railed, some who had been on their side turned against them. Seeing this, Sorceron said, 'I know that we have come to be a curse for you. It is because of us that you are suffering, I apologize. But we too are desperate, our kind is also dying. It is not that we knew what was to come. We did not even know that this planet existed, we drifted here by chance. I don't know if you will or can forgive us for what we have wrought upon you, but I assure you, that even if we die and our human race becomes extinct, we will save as many of you as we can. We will not allow your race to become extinct because of us. We are just two. But with your help, we can defeat the witches. So please, help us. Not to save humanity but to let us save you all. We will surrender if you do not help us.' Sorceron and Ricean stood and began to walk towards the door of the temple to surrender, they would wait for a moment. They hoped that the Resgords would help. They did not want to die such a death at the hands of the witches. Uproar ensued within the temple. Resgords began to talk to each other. Then, suddenly, the two outsiders heard a voice, 'Wait, wait. We will help you.' They continued. 'We now completely believe in the story you told us earlier. We were initially hesitant to help you, because some of us doubted the veracity of your cause. But, the arrival of the witches has proven it. You have taken a brave step to save your kind, and it does not matter what curse is upon us or what the consequences that we face, we will help you on your path. If there is any cause in this universe that is worthy of every praise and every curse, it is helping others. It is the greatest quality that the Creators have instilled in all beings. The cycle of life is possible only through this. Everyone now, and for the ages to come, will need help from others at some point during their lives. We were helped by the Creators. Being the first intelligent species of this universe, we have to help you. The witches may be powerful, but we have powers too. The Creators allowed us to keep our intelligence and with it, we will fight the witches.' Sorceron and Ricean were moved by their unconditional support. They had not expected the Resgords to fight for them. They made up their minds—they would not leave the remaining Resgords behind once the war ended. They would take them to a safe place before beginning their journey. Sorceron knew in his heart that even the Creators would not oppose his plans. Sorceron asked the Resgords to take him to his spacecraft. The spacecraft was incredibly powerful, and a single spacecraft of that make was enough to fight the thousands of spacecraft belonging to the witches. Schehil said that the spacecraft had been camouflaged by the hunters after Sorceron was captured. The witches could not have found it. And the war between the witches and the Resgords began. The Resgords gave up everything, just for the sake of saving humanity, a race they had never known about. This is why we are here now. However, they received their justice afterwards. We should be grateful to them, isn't that so?"

Mr Gregor paused. Sam immediately asked Mr Gregor, "What happens next, sir? What happens in the war? Did the Resgords and

Sorceron and Ricean survive the war? Were they able to find the Creators?"

Mr Gregor smiled. "Well, Sam, you have to wait to know the answers. You will be told more in the following term. You all are not ready yet. I'm very sorry, but I cannot continue further. I have other things to teach you all."

No one could believe what Mr Gregor had just said. They protested, "No sir! You can't do this to us." And shouts of, "We're eager to know what happened. Please, sir!"

"Don't do this, sir. The story just got more interesting," Mariane said.

"I understand your hastiness. But I cannot go on. First of all, our time today is up, and you are already late for lunch. Second, if I tell you the rest of the tale, I will not be able to teach you anything else and I will lose my job. Moreover, as I have already said—you are not ready. The next part of the story contains things you will not understand yet. So students, have patience."

All the students were disappointed on hearing this. They knew that it was going to be very difficult to concentrate on whatever came next., having listened to only half of such a gripping story. Sam looked especially disappointed. As Mr Gregor left, Mariane and John turned to Sam. While the other students had begun to move into conversations among themselves, Sam seemed to be lost in thought. John patted his back and said, "Hey! Lost somewhere?"

Sam smiled faintly and said, "I can't believe he left the story at that ..."

"Relax, Sam, we're all just as disappointed. In any case, it's just a story, and we are here to do so much more. Don't concentrate on this. Remember what Mr Gregor said?"

"Maybe they don't tell us the entire story so that we learn to develop patience?" Mariane added and John agreed.

"No guys, you're missing the point. It is not just a story. I felt something while I was listening to Mr Gregor. It felt like I had some relation to this story—as if Mr Gregor was talking about someone I knew."

Mariane laughed out loud and mocked Sam again, "Sam, you feel like you have a connection to everything in this universe. Have you asked yourself who you are? Maybe you are not from this universe?" She egged him on. "What would you do? Come on, Sam. The story may be true, or it may not, and even if it is true, it occurred ages before we were even born. How could you know someone from that time?"

Hearing this Sam laughed as well. "Mariane, why do you mock me so? I'm going to give you the beating of your life today."

With that, Sam began to chase Mariane around the room, trying his best to catch up to her. He forgot about the story and the doubts he had. Soon John joined the fun, teasing "Catch her, Sam. She always keeps mocking everyone, does not spare me either. Today, I will also eat a piece of the cake. Let's see where she runs today. Catch her."

The sapling of their friendship was now blooming, and they were joyous around each other. They were a joy to watch, even for the teachers and other staff at Volgarth. It was a delight to see a friendship bloom in a place where students are forced to concentrate only on their research.

The students soon left for lunch and the day continued as usual. Practical applications at their respective laboratories, and then, initial research on their topics. Classes ended and they returned to the Dorm.

As the evening sat on Tiron, Sam knew that whatever Mariane may say, the connection he felt was real. Volgarth and his own space within it were becoming more complicated with time. At that moment, he remembered his dream and that he was going to talk to Kasmuji. He had completely forgotten, being so deeply immersed in the history of humanity. He said to himself that he would definitely speak to Kasmuji about it the next day. As he went to the Dorm, the fear of the night and his dream returned to engulf him and drown out the joy of the day. But brave as he was, he kept fighting with himself.

The Walls And The Blood Orchids

It was a dark night and the students had taken their tea were working in their rooms. All of them pondered over the half-told story. Many thoughts bounded off the minds of every student who had been present at the class.; and within this maze of thoughts, one stood out. A dream, a nightmare—Sam's. As the night brought in its darkness, the fear grew stronger and stronger. He had not had a chance to speak to Kasmuji. Uncomfortable, he decided to go for a stroll outside. Sam and his friends had found the bell tower to be quite comfortable. They would often go there when they needed some air, especially Sam, as it had become his favourite place.

As he went down the stairs, he heard two voices talking to each other in the corridor near the dining hall. It was dark and Sam could not make out their faces. However, he from their voices, he gathered that one of them was a man and the other a woman. Initially, Sam thought he would ignore them. It was none of his business. He had to go in the opposite direction anyway.

But, as he came to the end of the stairs, he suddenly heard his name being spoken. This caught Sam's attention. Were they talking about him? What they could be talking about?

He walked closer towards the dining hall to listen. It was dark, more so than usual; it was otherwise always full of light. The dining hall, the stairs and the reception hall were all located on the ground floor. The entire floor only had few flickering candles, which let out a faint light. The glowing ancient writings on the walls of the reception hall proved to be another source of a faint, blurry sheen. Most of the corners of the hall were dark, and one could see another person only if they stood near the light. In the dark, the two figures could not see Sam approaching and so they did not stop their conversation. Sam was close enough to hear them clearly. He carefully hid behind a pillar. He could hear the male figure.

"Sam's dreams must have grown stronger by now. It's been quite some time since he's had the first."

"I can't say. Neither Sam nor his friends have reported any incidents of late. It might be that he is getting used to them and does not find it troublesome enough to complain," the lady spoke.

"Yes, maybe. But it's a matter of concern if the dreams have stopped. We have spent years waiting for this, and it will be blown to dust … I feel sorry for him too. He does not know anything. There were rumours yesterday. After Mr Gregor's class, he apparently said that he felt a connection while Mr Gregor was teaching them the history of humankind. I hope he is not moving too fast. We expected that to happen much later," the man said.

"I hope the dark shadow does not bother him much in his dreams. You must keep an eye on him. Give me every detail. I don't want to keep my eyes shut. He is very important to us. And remember, no one should know about this." The woman was about to continue when the man gestured at her to stop.

He had seen Sam's hand lurking behind the pillar. He knew that someone had heard them. The woman asked the man to run—"before anyone sees their faces".

The two ran in opposite directions. It was dark and Sam could only track one of them. Sam decided to follow the man. He could see him at some distance ahead of him. Running behind him, Sam began to shout, "Wait. Stop! Who are you?"

The man continued to run. The man ran as if he were familiar with the place and knew it very well. He ran towards the entrance of the Dorm and Sam followed. The man then took a U-turn and ran towards the door, on the opposite side of the dining hall. The ground floor was impossibly large, and the dark made it easier for the man to get away. Sam last saw him near the stairs, and then suddenly, he vanished into the dark. Sam could no longer see him. Panting, he veered to catch a glimpse of the man, and his eyes caught sight of a figure climbing the stairs. Sam ran towards it. Just as he was about to reach the figure, all the lights of the ground floor switched on. There was light everywhere. Shocked, Sam saw who the figure in front of him was. It was Jonathan. His could not believe his eyes. Why would Jonathan be talking about Sam? Confused, he asked, "Jonathan, why were you talking about me? Who was the lady you were talking to?"

Jonathan looked suspicious and confused when he heard Sam's question. Arrogant as he was, he replied rudely, "Have you lost your mind? I am just coming from the bell tower. What are you talking about?"

Sam did not believe it. He had seen the man disappear right at that spot!

"Don't lie to me. I know you were talking to someone about me. I heard you. I chased you and you disappeared into the dark near the stairs. Then I found you here, climbing the stairs," Sam said

"Sam! You seriously need to go to a doctor and get yourself checked. Your talk reeks of garbage, and they are increasing daily. I was in the bell tower. Don't you understand when I have already made it clear?" Jonathan replied.

As Sam was about to ask for more clarification, Jason interrupted from behind,

Sam was shocked at seeing Jason there. Jason's presence added to Sam's dismay.

"Where did you come from?" Sam asked in disbelief.

"I was with Jonathan. We went to the bell tower about an hour ago and have just returned. He was ahead of me and reached here first. What's wrong, Sam? You're sweating a lot."

Sam had to trust that it was not Jonathan, now that Jason had corroborated the story. However, there was still a doubt in his mind. Jonathan had earlier mentioned his dream. He would no longer contest Jonathan's claims, but Sam remained suspicious.

As Jonathan and Jason left towards their room, Sam went out towards the bell towers. On the top of the bell towers, the moon showered its faint light on the walls and the stars. The night sky could be seen through the tall window. Age had taken its toll on the bell tower and the window had transformed into a huge hole that reached its very top. The bell tower perfectly resembled a space observatory, with a telescope mounted on one of its walls.

Sam sat at the very top, looking at stars. His life had become so complicated. Wasn't it enough? The nightmares, the mysteries of Volgarth, the histories—was it not enough already? Now he had heard two figures speaking about him and his dreams! He looked towards the stars and thought of his parents. He had never even seen them; he'd had to go through so much to reach this place. Everything might have been so much simpler if only his parents had been with him. All these years of loneliness had not affected him as much as they were now; he was beginning to realize that there was a deep void in his life. There were tears in his eyes. As he was trying to gather his thoughts to have the courage to face all the challenges that lay in front of him, his silence was broken by Mariane and John.

John had gone to check on Sam in his room and ask after his well-being. He had noticed how disappointed Sam had been when the story was left unfinished. John knew about the dreams as well. When he could not find Sam in his room, he had felt slightly worried. So John had gone and informed Mariane.

They'd both known where to find Sam. They had run to the bell towers. On the way, John told Mariane about the dream Sam had had the last night. They knew that their friend needed them. On reaching the top of the bell tower, Mariane breathed a sigh of relief, "I told you, John. He would be here, looking at the stars, trying to find a relation to it; our typical Mr Curious." She followed with a giggle.

"Hey, Mariane—not now! Sam is really in need of some comfort.

You know what he is going through! Can't you stop mocking him for once?" John said seriously.

"Am I talking to you, John?" Mariane looked away from him. "Why are you interrupting talk between the two of us?"

Sam interrupted with a laugh, "Yes John, how dare you interrupt Mariane, the great mockingbird? Let her continue."

John laughed out loud. In a hurt voice, Mariane continued, "You guys! How can you call me a mockingbird? I just joke around to keep things light and cheerful—not serious."

"Oh look, Sam, someone just got serious. What will you do, mockingbird, fly away?" John egged her on.

"No, John," she replied smartly. "I won't fly away as easily. I will first poke you with my beak and then fly away." All three of them started to laugh and they hugged each other.

Still hugging, Mariane spoke again, "Sam, we know that what you are going through is tough. Don't we always tell you to come to us if you have any problem? We are your friends for life, Sam. Don't come all by yourself to this bell tower and sit in your solitude. You'll feel worse. We know you like this place. If you feel like coming here, tell us, and we will join you, but please, don't make yourself feel so alone and lonely. It might not be safe here. Remember what happened here the first time? Someone was watching us. What if you are attacked? We really are concerned about you and we really feel bad when you make yourself feel so alone."

Hearing Mariane's words, Sam responded quickly, "No friends, I didn't mean anything like that. Please don't misunderstand. You guys are the only people that bring me any comfort in this place. I know I can share everything with you, and believe me, I do share everything with you. It's just that ... as days are passing, my life is becoming more and more complicated."

Sam told John and Mariane everything that had happened before he had come to the bell tower. He then continued, "All these events … I just found myself thinking of my parents a lot and I came here by myself. I have never seen them, you know. I don't know their names, but whenever I look up at the night sky and the stars, I always feel that they are with me, looking after me from somewhere far. All my loneliness dissipates. I feel like they come down from the stars and cuddle with me. That's all, friends. This is why I came here today alone. It's just that my life would have been so different if they had been with me …"

"Sam, we understand what's in your heart. It's okay. Mariane was just trying her best. Just remember, we are always with you—no matter what. We are not just friends; we are a family. Put away all your worries and let's go now. It will be time for dinner soon," John said

Having spoken about what he had kept pent up for so long, Sam felt cheered. He decided to do something fun. He said, "Let's race. From here to the dorm. Let us see who wins."

John replied, "Such a great idea, Sam! It will be fun, and the race will be only between you and me, because Mariane here would not stand a chance. Only if she decides to fly might she stand a chance."

Both John and Sam began to laugh at her. Mariane turned red. Her anger knew no bounds. She replied angrily, "I will show you both who wins. Now stop chattering and let's start the race."

They all took their positions and the race began. They puffed and panted and reached the dorm—and all three of them close to reaching the point together. But Mariane reached there first, followed by Sam, and then John. Laughing and giggling on the way to their rooms, John crashed against someone. Immediately, he began to apologize and saw that it was Kasmuji. Delighted at seeing him at this hour, Sam asked, "Kasmuji! What are you doing here at this time?"

Kasmuji responded seriously, "Why, Sam? I am a teacher. I can go wherever I want at whichever time I prefer. You have any problem with that?"

And the smiles on the three faces vanished. Seeing this, Kasmuji burst out in throaty laughter and said, "Oh, you guys. I was just kidding. I had some work with Miss Hollande. Where are you guys coming from this late?"

"We went to see the stars in the bell tower," Mariane replied.

"Oh! The stars! Interesting. One day you will go among those very stars in your quest to discover the magical world."

While Kasmuji waxed about the stars, Sam had realized that he had wanted to talk to Kasmuji about his dream. He thought he'd ask now, before it was too late, and forgotten again. He said, "Kasmuji, I had to discuss an important matter with you. I thought I would tell you in class today, but I forgot. Can you please give me some of your time? It's really important."

"Of course, Sam. I am free now. Let's go to your room and we can discuss it there. We still have about half an hour before dinner."

In Sam's room, Sam started to narrate his dream. He told Kasmuji about how it all started on his very first night in Volgarth, about the dark shadow and the two figures, the forbidden forests. Hesitant to speak his mind, Sam preserved and told Kasmuji that he had seen him in one of his dreams, along with Miss Hollande and Mr Esdorg, all his friends and colleagues. The dark shadow had come and engulfed every one of them. Sam continued, saying, "At first, I thought that it was just a normal nightmare but then it began to happen every night. Each night that passed, the visions and images in the dream have only grown stronger. I've seen so much. Last night, it was the worst—faces of the two bright figures, who told me about hard work and my destiny, they had been waiting they said. I saw two sides to the forbidden forest. I saw John and the dark shadow again. John was like a guide. I saw the Volgarth, its fourth pillar and a heap of skulls and bones inside the pillar ..."

Sam continued and filled in all the details, ending his narrative with the cliff and his fall through the light.

Kasmuji observed the confusion and fear on Sam's face. He knew that Sam was scared. Gathering that the situation was fragile, he said politely, "Sam, don't be as upset as you are. We all have nightmares. I understand that there are many questions regarding these dreams. They are strange things that began after you've come here. But, maybe, it's just a coincidence. We all have nightmares at different stages of our lives. I had them when I was a little kid. You have them now. It must be hard for you to believe that it's just a coincidence—but let me explain it to you. Tell me, Sam, why did you join the IMMR?"

"To find the magical world," Sam replied immediately.

Kasmuji asked again, "Now tell me why you want to find the magical world?"

Sam replied, "Because I am curious to know if such a world really exists and if we can find it. If we do, the universe will take a completely different turn. After having come here, I also get a feeling that I have a connection with the magical world, which has made me even more curious."

Kasmuji smiled and asked, "And Sam, do you believe that it is your destiny to find that world?"

Sam replied, "I have always believed that destiny is shaped by our hard work. The universe always gives the most to the one who deserves it. In order to make something your destiny, you will first have to work hard to achieve it. Only if you have worked hard enough, more than anyone else pursuing the same destiny, will you be destined to achieve the highest."

Kasmuji was moved by Sam's beliefs. He said, "I am proud of you Sam. Your thoughts are so noble. You remind me of someone I once knew." His eyes began to well up.

After a brief pause, Kasmuji continued, "Okay, coming back to your dream. Now look at it this way. You came to Volgarth to find the magical world, and the dreams began as soon as you reached here. You said that the dream talks about hard work, right? You also find two sides of a forest? It might be trying to tell you something.

He continued. "You must work hard and find the other side of the forest, which may very well be the magical world itself! Your destiny is in your hands, after all. Your dream reminds you that there will be challenges in your path. The dark shadow that you see symbolizes the challenges you will face, and your friend and teachers show you that you will have their support in your journey. Don't be afraid of nightmares, Sam. Make your fear into a strength. Accept whatever you see and interpret your nightmare positively."

Sam thought for a while about the things Kasmuji had said. Kasmuji's way of interpreting Sam's dreams in a positive way started making sense to him. After a brief pause, Sam replied, "Kasmuji. Thank you very much. I had never thought of my nightmares in this manner. It makes it wholly new. You are right. The dreams must be occurring to make me aware of my responsibilities here and my ultimate goal."

Smiling, Sam felt that Kasmuji had cleared all his doubts. He was happy and could finally relax. Kasmuji began to rise and said, "Sam, it's time for dinner. I must leave now. Come let us walk together to the dining hall."

Even though Kasmuji knew that he had been able to convince and comfort Sam, a sense of tension lingered on in his mind and reflected upon his face.

They left the room and went to the dining hall. Kasmuji greeted Miss Hollande and left with her. All evening, Sam breathed easier. When he went to bed, he was now no longer scared of his nightmares. Kasmuji had planted a very positive seed. He closed his eyes, ready to face whatever may come.

As the days went by, Sam and his friends learnt many new things. Soon enough, their first term at Volgarth was about to end. The classes had become more interesting with time and they had gotten a taste of what lay in the real world. Their experiments went smoothly, and many of the students had already begun their actual research and achieved great leaps already. Time had come to a close, and it was not far off that the students would be taken to field trips to various corners of the universe, to give them guided working experience on-site. They would learn more there, see how they have to work and tackle various glitches that often occur while on-site.

Meanwhile, the friendship between Sam, John and Mariane had grown stronger still. They were inseparable and high achievers, always outperforming the other students in group activities. But otherwise, they had also found a sense for mischief. They would often jump out at night and scare everyone or spend all night sitting in the bell towers, observing the sky. Sam's dreams continued every night, but he read into them as if they were prophetic and worked harder every day to make his goal his destiny. he

He still had doubted the various elements of Volgarth and wanted answers and was especially desperate wanted to find out the secrets about the four pillars, the mysterious door, the wall and the monkey orchids. Volgarth's mystery and its rules prevented them from going out and exploring those places. However, now that they had grown accustomed to the place and were no longer as afraid, they were ready to set out.

It was a full-moon night and most of the scholars were sitting in the bell tower, having eaten their dinner with relish. Jane, Jonathan, Jason, and Juliana and had joined the trio. As they were fooling around, Sam said, "Guys, our first term is about to end, and we still don't know anything about so much here. Don't you think, before the first term ends, we should decipher some of the secrets of this place?"

Mariane, uncertain as to what Sam had planned, replied smartly,

"Mr Curious, we are not as curious as you are. We already have lots of other things to do. The term is ending, and the workload is heavy. Moreover, who would want to drag in more trouble?"

Sam smirked at Mariane and said, "What's the point of asking the mockingbird anything. You just know how to run away."

Marianne scoffed, and seeing this, Sam gestured to the others and asked, "What about you guys? Don't you ever feel like knowing about the mysterious door, or the wall, or the monkey orchids, or at least the pillars?"

"We do want to know. We are all curious," John said, and everybody else nodded.

Excited by this unanimity, Sam got up and said, "I have a plan. Let's go near the wall today and see what happens. We were being strictly told not to go towards the wall at night. But there is a full moon today and we will be able to see the path."

Everybody agreed, except for Mariane. She kept saying that it was not safe, asking what would happen if something went wrong. But nobody was in the mood to listen to her—they all wanted to explore the wall and the monkey orchids.

But as they all supported Sam, she had to finally agree. They decided they would set out at midnight. But they wanted to avoid being seen by Miss Hollande and had to come up with a way to get past her. Miss Hollande who even in her sleep remained conscious enough to wake up at the drop of a pin on the floor. Although the ground floor housed all the other staff of the dorm, Miss Hollande was the one to be wary of.

At midnight, the seven of them tiptoed out of their rooms. They had to be as quiet as they could until they reached the main door of the dorm. Sam, quickly looking back to see that all of them were there was satisfied that they had managed to all approach the door together. Upon reaching the door, Jonathan seemed to have realized something and whispered, "We have come this far but does anyone know how to open the door? It must be locked."

At this, they all sighed. They realized that none of them had thought this far ahead, and despite all their planning, would now have to turn back. But to their amusement, Sam spoke up, "I know how to get the door open. I have been trying to get past this door for quite some time now."

Everybody looked at Sam in disbelief. John, hopeful now, asked, "You have been trying to get out to the wall for quite some time now? You never even told us."

To this, Sam began to fiddle with the lock on door, replying, "Yes, I have been trying to get out and you all will be amazed to know that I have found a way to open this door. One day as I was coming through to open the door, I saw two people near the door, opening it and going to the other side. As I hid behind the pillars, I observed them and overheard one of them talk about a book in a secret chamber in the library which contained the methods to open the door. It took me a while to find the secret chamber in the library and the book. The book said that you have to turn the knob of the door in ten special directions with each direction representing a special degree of the position of Tiron with respect to the star Sun. And if you can master your hands enough to be able to turn the knob in those precise degrees, the door will open. It also said that, in order for the door to open, you have to be with people who will never leave you alone and whom you can trust with your life. Now, let's see if you guys will ever leave me alone." Sam smiled as he continued turning the knob of the door.

After some time, the door opened. They hoped that the door would not creak when they closed it.

As the door opened, it brought a sense of joy to Sam. He knew that the people he was with will be his true friends for time immemorial and he can always count upon them. Now that the secret book and the secret of opening the door had given him the proof, he sighed with a sense of relief in his eyes.

After having snuck out, Jane said, "Ah, Sam, you do know how to unlock it from the outside, right?"

Sam giggled at this and said, "We won't close the door completely." Saying this, he put a small rock carefully between the doors to prevent its closing.

Jane smiled, but the concern still clouded her face.

"Is it safe this way? What if someone notices that the door is open and locks it from the inside? We'll be trapped here," Jason said, picking up on Jane's concern

"No one will notice. You're all getting scared without a reason. Come, let's go to the wall," Sam hastily replied.

They all headed towards the wall. The wall ran across one side of Volgarth and completely covered it. They had to walk a short distance from the main door to reach the wall. However, the path that ran parallel to the wall was like a maze. The moonlight lit the path. Since it had been a while since they had last gone through it, they could have gotten lost easily. But Sam had the foresight to have taken a map of Volgarth from the library, which he carried. Sam led the others. They recollected the areas they had crossed, such as the airfield on their first day in Tiron, gradually. As they moved ahead, they could see the monkey orchids on top of the wall.

The night kept growing darker, and the moon was hiding behind the dark clouds. At that moment, John pointed out, "Look at those orchids! They're turning red."

With the darkening night, the orchids were changing colour, turning red. Suddenly, the moon disappeared behind some clouds and some of Sam's friends began to feel scared. It almost looked as if the orchids were staring right at them. Mariane voiced their fears, "Let's go back, guys.

It's getting dark and we can hardly see anything. We should not stay long. It's getting scary."

Sam was quick to interrupt Mariane. "Don't worry, Mariane, I've brought flashlights for all of us. I had a feeling that something like this might happen. Here, take one." He took out the flashlights from his bag and distributed them among everyone. They switched the lights on and moved ahead. They reached a point from where they could see the four pillars of Volgarth. They decided to stop and catch their breath for a while. While they stood there looking at the four pillars, Sam said, "Friends, have you ever wondered what might be inside those pillars? It's been a while here, and no teacher has mentioned anything about those pillars."

Prompted, Juliana replied, "I sometimes do. Look how they stand in the night sky, rising from the ground—like knights protecting their king."

"Indeed. I always imagine weird things inside those pillars. Sometimes I wonder if my dreams are real," Sam murmured to himself as he stared towards the pillars.

As Juliana asked Sam what he had just said, Jane suddenly spoke, "Have you guys realized how far we have come from the dorm? Look at the lights from the pillars. They are hardly reaching us. I have this strange feeling as if something is not right here. We should go back"

Mariane grabbed this opportunity and said, "Yes, yes. We should return immediately. We have come a long way. We must not go any further. Those orchids are giving me goosebumps."

Sam did not want to go, nor did some of the others, including John. They had taken such risks to reach here, and they did not want to leave without having found at least a single answer. They insisted that Mariane and the others stay a little bit longer and began to move further ahead. The path was now getting more and more twisted and curved. The puzzle of the maze was becoming tougher. The map had shown the way up till then, so they continued to follow it. They could see the treetops of the forbidden forests on the other side of the wall. After walking for some time, Mariane had had enough. She stopped and said, "I don't know about you guys, but I am going back. We have come a long way in this darkness to a forbidden place and I am not going one step further."

Sam knew that any further would be too much to ask of his friend. He was not satisfied but he knew that his friend was scared and wanted to go back. Supporting Mariane, he said, "All right friends, let's go back. I guess we are not getting any answers tonight." He was disappointed.

Sam walked behind them as they started to head towards the dorm. He wanted to make sure that he could see everyone, and none would get lost. He kept yelling directions from behind them, and their journey back seemed just as smooth as the one they'd taken a few hours ago. But suddenly, Sam's voice could no longer be heard. They thought they were on the right path, and Sam had decided to stop directing them. But after a considerable time, John decided to call out to Sam. He heard nothing. Sam was nowhere to be seen. He shouted at the others.

"Stop guys! Sam is missing."

Everyone stopped in their tracks. They all turned around and could not see Sam anywhere. They focused their flashlights in every direction and could only see a faint mist. Sam was nowhere.

Tense, they started to shout out and call his name. They considered it and thought that Sam might just be playing a prank, so they pleaded that he stop goofing around. But soon, they realized that something was wrong. They walked back the way they had come, looking for Sam and it was not long before they found the map lying in the ground. They immediately knew that something had seriously gone wrong. Mariane began to panic and cried out, "I warned you all that it was dangerous. But no one listened. Now see what has happened. How will we find Sam now? What will say? Do any of you even know if how we can get out of here?"

Uncertain and worried, they decided to go little further in search of Sam. They did not find Sam anywhere. Jonathan stepped up and said, "We cannot change what has happened. We don't know where Sam is, and we don't know if we are safe here. We must be smart now. I suggest that we return to the Dorm and tell Miss Hollande about what has happed. We alone cannot find Sam here. We have the map, let's use it to go back and tell her. If Sam is in trouble, they are our best option to help him."

Everyone agreed and decided to return to the Dorm. Their heartbeats fast, they could not stop thinking about what could have happened to Sam. The darkness and those red orchids terrified them more than before. They moved ahead while holding onto each other's hands, praying that they reach the dorm safely and in time to save Sam.

When they had almost reached, they all felt strange, like someone was chasing after them. As they looked back, they saw that the red orchids had were now moving! They had covered the entire path and were moving fast towards them. The orchids looked redder now, like they were made of blood.

They started to run as fast as they could. They could see the dorm get closer. They ran in its direction. The orchids were chasing them like they were prey. In their hurry, they dropped their flashlights but somehow, managed to reach close to the door. As soon as they were about to push it open, a strong gust of wind blew, causing the stone to move and the door closed on them.

John, Jonathan, Jane, Mariane and Juliana saw the door closing, but they could not do anything. Their fears knew no bounds. The door was closed, and the red orchids were almost at their feet. They did not know what to do. They started banging on the door hoping that someone would hear it and open it—but it was late, and everyone was asleep. The orchids were so close. If the door was not opened immediately, no one knew what would happen to them.

They hit the door harder, screaming. The red orchids were at their feet and their tangled roots were trying to hold on to them. They were pulling with great force. Jonathan, John, and Jason each had a stick in their hands and were trying to resist the orchids, smacking them as hard as they could.

But the number of orchids kept increasing. Suddenly, Jane's hand caught hold of a bell on the door. She caught hold of it and started to swing at it. The bell was connected directly to Miss. Hollande's room, and as it started ringing, it reverberated through the entire ground floor. Miss Hollande immediately woke up and knew that something was wrong. She hurried towards the door. As she opened the door, she could see Jane. Jane was there sitting at the doorstep, terrified with her head in her hands. As Miss Hollande touched her, she looked up and began to wail, "Miss Hollande! Please help us. They will take us away. Please."

Miss Hollande looked around but saw no one there. Something terribly wrong had happened, she felt and she hastily asked Jane, "Jane, dear, what happened? What are you talking about? I don't see anyone."

Surprised, Jane looked around her. There was no one. Her friends were no longer with her. When the door had opened, Jane had felt that she still had time. But they were gone.

By then, all the other staff at the Dorm had also heard the ruckus and had come rushing. Jane started to cry.

She told Miss Hollande everything: why they had gone out so late at night, how Sam had disappeared, and about the blood-red orchids and how John, Jonathan, Mariane, Juliana and Jason were no longer there.

Miss Hollande immediately seemed to know what had happened. She understood the depth of the problem. She said, "You were being strictly prohibited from there. Were you all out of your minds? Do you know what you have done?"

She instructed the staff to take Jane inside, and then to the medical assistance room. She herself rushed to inform the others. She informed the director and Kasmuji, asking them to spread the word among all the teachers, students, and everyone at Volgarth.

Everyone rushed out as fast as they could. Sirens were rung and an emergency was declared. Volgarth would not sleep that night. The confused students did not know what was happening, but they were asked to remain alert and not to come to the ground floor at any cost.

Meanwhile, Sam found himself lying in the mud when his eyes opened. His head felt heavy and his vision was blurry. He did not know what had happened. The last thing he remembered was returning to the Dorm with his friends. He tried to lift himself up from the mud, but he found that he could barely stand. It felt like he was inside one of his dreams.

Drenched in mud, he somehow stood up. His vision was still blurry. He looked everywhere and could see only darkness. There was nothing else. Slowly, as he walked, he began to hear strange sounds and screaming. *"Where am I? Where are my friends?"* He had no idea of where he was going or where he was.

After having walked some distance, he felt like someone was behind him. He looked back to see a red orchid soaring high in the sky. It was staring at Sam. The orchid suddenly grew branches, and in a flash, the branches reached out and tried to grab Sam. Sam was taken aback and fell on the ground, into the mud again. He realized that something very bad had happened and he was in a lot of trouble. The branches reached out and Sam crawled in the mud as fast as he could. *Why is it after me?* He hurried up to get back on his feet, and ran, without looking back. After some time, he stopped. He could hear his heart beating fast. The orchid was not behind him. Again, he tried to discern his surroundings and again saw only darkness. He was cold. His mud-drenched clothes made him shiver. He did not know what was happening. *What is that orchid? Why is it so dark here?*

Despite the cold and his fear, he knew that he would have to control himself and act carefully. He knew that he could not take any decisions as he was unable to reason with anything he was seeing. As he wondered and tried to figure it out, the sky started to clear, and the moon came out again. It was a little brighter than before and he could see the tall trees around him. He looked down and saw that the ground was muddy. He was standing in a small and muddy, open space surrounded by trees. Sam decided to move forward even though he did not know where he was. The moonlight made it easier for him.

Sam carefully put one step in front of another. He trudged into the dense forest and kept going. His legs were so stiff he could hardly move. He kept walking for what seemed like a long time. His heart told him to stop. The forest felt airless, it smelled of decay. Trees were decomposing in the mud that beneath his feet. Sam could not decide which direction to take or which direction he had come from. He kept stumbling, and he got ahead by holding on to one tree after another. But he kept going deeper into the forest where the mud was denser, and it made walking more difficult. Suddenly, he saw a small opening in the forest. His mind cleared as the sight of light. He increased his pace and tried to get out of the forest as fast as possible.

When Sam felt joy and relief after having reached the open space. But it only lasted a moment. As he looked around himself, he realized that he had returned to the same muddy place from where he had started. He panicked. He did not know what to do. He was trapped. His body was now getting numb. He knew that the cold was taking a toll on his body. He was wet, disheartened, and hopeless. And thought the orchid further terrified him.

Amidst all these feelings, he decided to wait at the edge of the open space and rest. His mind was still in a state of shock, and he could barely feel any strength inside him. He sat under a tree near the edge. It was the only space from where he could see the sky. But there were no stars in the sky. Feeling a mixture of sorrow and fear, he fell asleep, hoping that someone would come through the sky to his rescue.

CHAPTER 8

The Holidays

The first term at Volgarth ended amidst much tension. The students were glad to be able to leave and were getting ready for their vacation. Glad go back to their homes and meet their families, one by one, the students said their goodbyes to their friends and teachers.

Sam had packed his bags for Earth. Although he had no one back on his planet, he wanted to go and live somewhere for a few calmer days. Sam and his friends—John, Mariane, Jane, Jonathan, Jason, and Juliana—had made plans to enjoy their holidays at the planet, Entertrox. Entertrox was a famous tourist attraction and was known for the fun and entertainment it provided. 'The wolf pack' as they had been dubbed after their recent dangerous adventure, were to take along Patrick and Indiana, Jane's group mates, who had agreed to join them. They decided to meet at the Inter Universal Space Station in a week to begin their journey.

It was time for the friends to bid farewell. However short the time spent away from each other would be, it was going to be hard for them to stay away after having gone through so much together. They stood together at the airfield in Volgarth. Kasmuji, Mr Gregor and Miss Hollande had come to see them off. One after another, their LMVs arrived. Jonathan's was the first to arrive. He hugged everyone and went in. In the last year, the arrogant Jonathan had also begun to show his softer side, full of affection and care for his friends. Although he always tried to maintain character, at moments like this, he could not hide it and his eyes welled up. Jason was the next to go, and one by one, they all left. Sam and Jane were the only ones left. Their LMV's had not arrived yet. Meanwhile, Kasmuji approached Sam and asked, "Sam, will you both be comfortable staying here by yourselves? We teachers have some things to take care of and are getting late. Will you be comfortable if we go ahead?"

Sam replied, "Of course, Kasmuji. We can wait here. The other students are also here. You guys can go. Don't worry, and thanks for coming to see us off."

The teachers hugged Sam and Jane and left. Before leaving, Miss Hollande smiled in her tight-lipped manner, grave and concerned, and said, "Enjoy your holidays. Don't do stupid things like you did a few months ago. You may have earned the name of a wolf pack, but don't behave like one in Entertrox."

Sam and Jane both laughed, realizing what trouble they had caused. They waved as the teachers left the airfield.

The airfield was going to be busy that day. It is full of students waiting for their vehicles to arrive so they could ride home. The many LMVs looked like bees swarming in the sky. Thanks to the advanced air-traffic-control, and the manoeuvrability of the LMV's, it was well managed. Sam recalled an old uncle who lived in his neighbourhood, who would often speak about the various air crashes that used to occur in the early days of its development. "Air traffic control was such a headache back then," he would say. "But now, it has become so easy. The controls are all automatic and not a single crash has been reported in many decades."

How far the human race had come! They could control almost everything perfectly. In his thoughts, Sam completely forgot that Jane was with him. He looked at her and said, "I am sorry. I almost forgot that you were here and was deep in thought. You must be getting bored."

Jane said, "No, not at all, Sam. I was observing you. No wonder Mariane keeps calling you names. You seem to always be lost in your own world." There was a vague smile on her face, as if she wanted to laugh but was controlling it.

Sam understood that she too was pulling his leg. He sighed and said, "Now you please don't start pulling my leg too. I was thinking about the air traffic control and how it makes so many LMVs fly together. At the same time, in the same place."

Jane smiled and said, "I was just kidding Sam. Don't get too serious.

Tell me something about yourself. We have known each other for almost a year now, and I never had a chance to ask you anything yourself."

Sam was lost again, but this time, it was Jane's smile that occupied his thoughts. He had spent so much time with her. But, only today had he noticed her smile so closely. Sam felt that this, this may be one of his most beautiful moments. Jane waved her hands in front of his eyes and burst out in laughter,

"Ha ha! Sam, you are unbelievable. You were lost again somewhere."

Sam realized that she had caught him staring at her. Blushing red, he said softly, "No, I was not lost anywhere. You were asking about me, right? Well, I am from Earth and I, I live there ... I am from there ... I am a student of mystic sciences and I love the subject ..."

Jane could not stop her laughter, "What has happened to you, Sam? You are acting weird today. You look so funny like this."

She had noticed Sam staring at her. She knew something was happening and she liked it too. But wanting it to continue, she decided to pretend that she hadn't understood and went with the flow.

Laughter and cheer rang out everywhere. Although the students were leaving their friends and going home, they would be meeting their families and loved ones after a long time. The atmosphere was cheerful.

Suddenly, there was a loud boom. An explosion had occurred in one of the LMVs!

The explosion soon triggered off a series of explosions in several other LMVs in the sky. The explosions were so powerful that it sent shockwaves throughout the airfield. As the burning debris started to fall towards the waiting area, Sam held on to Jane's hand and they ran to take cover.

They ran into a tunnel that had probably been constructed to solve the water-logging problem in the airfield. It began on the surface and the tunnel went few feet under the ground. Debris fell like burning meteors, causing more explosions wherever they landed. The entire airfield caught fire.

Sam and Jane were in shock. So many lives must have been lost, all their friends. They couldn't do anything to save them. They felt helpless.

Volgarth was again in a state of emergency. Sirens sounded. Fire-control spacecraft had all been in the airfield, and most of them had been destroyed in the fire. The remaining could not fly due to the excessive heat that had been caused by the fire. Fire-protection spacecraft were called in from nearby planets. But the nearest planet was an hour away. Within the hour, the entire airfield would be burned to ashes and there would be no survivors.

Finally, the authorities at Volgarth decided to use traditional means to quell the fire. They had a few older fire trucks and decided to use them. The trucks reached the site and started to douse the fire. The students who had managed to escape the airfield too started to work alongside them to bring the fire under control. The airfield had fire extinguishers and water channels inside, but the fire had been so sudden and powerful that no one had even a chance to use them.

The students decided to use the main water channel to the airfield to get the water. They bypassed the main pipe and attached it to several other pipes, all finally connecting to the airfield. They started to use those pipes to spray water on the fire.

The fire truck crew and the students were desperate. The fire kept growing and torching the spacecraft that had been kept idly aside. The explosions continued. All of them knew that if the fire was not controlled immediately all the spacecraft would blow up and this would result in a graver disaster.

Relentlessly, they continued to douse the airfield with, which began to flow through the tunnels after a while. Soon enough, the water had travelled into the tunnel in which Sam and Jane were hiding. Concerned, they realized that the tunnel they were hiding in would soon be flooded.

The fire was still blazing, and it would not be possible to escape through the other side. They decided to follow the tunnel and to try to find the other end. The water level was increasing and was at their feet now. Sam and Jane started to walk briskly in the opposite direction.

The tunnel seemed to be quite long. Soon the water rose up to their knees, and the flow had created a strong current and it was getting difficult to keep standing, let alone walk. But they moved ahead, holding onto each other's hands. Finally, they saw the opening of the tunnel. The water was at their chest, and they were almost swimming in it. They hurried towards the opening and they came out near a small river. Wet and cold, but they had reached the river, and Sam said, "This place is full of surprises. Now we have found a river that none of us knew about."

Jane was more concerned about returning as they did not know where they were. She said, "Sam, forget about the river. We must find a way to go back. The tunnel was quite long, and we must have come far."

They looked around and saw a hill before them. Sam thought for a while and said, "The tunnel must have been built beneath this hill. That means we have to cross the hill in order to reach the airfield."

Jane saw that he was right, and they began their climb. The basin of the river was covered in a thick forest, and all the bushes and branches tangled in their feet and clothes. Moreover, they were afraid that they would find dangerous creatures lurking—even poisonous snakes. After a short hike, they reached the top of the hill. Although the landscape was filled with tall grass, the smoke from the airfield could be seen from there. They knew where they had to go.

They walked through the grass, not realizing that it was as strong and sharp as saws. They were cut and stung everywhere. Their entire bodies were bruised by the needles of the grass. Sam decided to walk ahead to clear a path for Jane. Taking off his shirt, he wrapped it around both his arms, and keeping his arms in front of him, he went through the saw grass.

Some distance later they were at the airfield, but on the opposite side of the fire, which was still blazing. They had to go around the airfield now to reach the other side. Until the fire would be completely extinguished, no one would come to the opposite side or spot them there.

But they were exhausted, and as they held on to the fence that barricaded the airfield, Jane sat down and said, "Sam, I cannot walk any more. I don't have the energy to go around the airfield. I am not moving."

The area around the airfield was covered with the same, dangerous grass and it was a risk to go around the airfield. They had reached the airfield after many travails and did not want to leave it out of their sight. They decided to wait where they were, at least till the fire was under control. They hoped someone would come to find them.

While the two of them sat near the fence, Jane came up to Sam and hugged him. She softly said, "I am so scared, Sam."

Sam held her tightly and comforted her, "Don't worry, I am here with you. We are near the airfield. Sooner or later someone will find us."

They sat there, gazing quietly at the destruction that had unfolded before their eyes. They knew that many students could not have survived it. They were lucky, as tired as they were. In a few moments, they heard a growling sound from the sky. They looked up and saw spacecraft hovering around the airfield.

Help had arrived. The spacecraft from the neighbouring planets had come to Volgarth's rescue. The men began to spray dry ice on the fire. Gradually, more and more fire rescue ships drew closer and worked to spray every inch of the raging fire. The fire was finally under control. The destruction it had left behind could now be seen through the smoke.

Sam and Jane heard footsteps approaching them. They knew that someone had spotted them and had come to their rescue. As the smoke in front of them cleared, they could see people running towards them.

They felt relieved.

As the people approached nearer, they saw Kasmuji and a few of their friends. They cut through the fence and brought in Sam and Jane, who were then immediately rushed to the medical emergency van. They had bruises all over them. Sam had wounds all over his arms. The saw grass had done their work. Both of his arms were covered in bandages, and ointments were applied on some other scraped parts of his body. Jane had minor cuts on her hands and legs. After the bandages had been applied, Jane walked up to Sam and said, "Thank you, Sam." Tears started to roll down her cheeks when she saw the state Sam was in. She could stop herself, she hugged Sam and started crying loudly.

Seeing her cry so much, Sam lifted her head, rubbed her tears and said, "Hey, why are you crying? It's okay, I am alright. Stop crying now. Our work is not finished yet. We have to help the others who are trapped inside. We cannot rest now. Our friends need us."

As soon as he said this, Sam realized that they had completely forgotten about the wolf pack. He immediately looked at Jane

"Do you know what happened to John, Mariane, Jonathan, Jason, Juliana, Partick, and Indiana? Are they safe? Did their LMVs lift off before the explosion?" A worried Sam asked.

Jane as Sam was worried too. They had no idea what happened to their friends from the wolf pack. They began to search for Kasmuji or any other teacher to find out answers but could not find anyone at the vicinity. They were worried and tensed to their bones.

Sam and Jane were offered new clothes as theirs were wet. They put them on and went to help the others. Suddenly, Kasmuji came and said, "Where are you going? You need to rest."

Seeing Kasmuji, Sam, and Jane showed a sigh of relief.

"Are John, Mariane, Jonathan, Jason, Juliana, Partick, and Indiana safe? Do you know what happened to them?" Sam asked.

"They are all right. All of their LMVs had left the airfield before the explosion. They are probably in their homes by now. I will update you as soon as I hear from them," Kasmuji responded.

This brought about a huge relief to Sam and Jane. Knowing that their friends from the wolf pack were safe. But they also knew that not all the students were as lucky. They still had many friends who probably have lost their lives, are missing, or are injured. They could not wait but go help all the people in need.

"We are going to help the others; they need it more than we need our rest. We know that we are short of staff," Sam asked Kasmuji.

Kasmuji did not stop them and allowed them to join the other rescue workers. All of Volgarth worked together. All the staff, the teachers, the remaining students, even the director was working with them to help as many people as they can. They were going to every corner of the airfield to look for survivors. The Life Detection Machines were used to their full capabilities to find any life below the debris and everyone was lending a helping hand in clearing out the debris to extract the survivors. The casualties were high, and they needed to find and treat everyone they could before it was too late. There was no one too big or too small in that moment.

When they entered the airfield, Sam and Jane were told to search for any living persons. This was a difficult thing for both Sam and Jane. They had never seen such chaos before, let alone any dead person. To look through the debris using the Life Detection machines and see for dead and living people sent chills down their spines. But, both of them knew that it was not the time to feel pity and get scared. They had to keep their emotions aside and actively look for any living person who needs help. They could see debris lying on the ground; they had never seen anything like it before. It was such a grim site to see. Among the debris, they wondered whether they would come across the ashes of their friends who had been burnt alive. They shuddered. As they walked past the debris, someone called out and said, "I know it's hard. It is hard for every one of us. But don't stroll here. Someone alive might need your help desperately."

This urgency was enough to bring Sam and Jane back to their senses. They began to search every nook and corner; they looked underneath the debris to find anyone who may be alive and injured. As they scanned through the debris, they could see many of their fellow friends lying lifeless underneath a pile of rocks and vehicle parts. This site was so grim and painful for them. They could not hold up their tears as the Life Detection Machines flashed red indicating no signs of life. The entire evening passed and to their surprise, Sam and Jane did not find anyone alive. They returned to the rendezvous point. Outside the airfield, they met Miss Hollande. She said that the search crew had looked everywhere and all those alive had been taken to receive medical assistance. Jane seemed satisfied with the news, but Sam was not as hopeful. His heart did not agree with Miss Hollande's words. He felt that still someone still needed his help. He said, "Miss Hollande, can you give us permission to search one last time? I have a feeling that someone might be still there."

Looking at how desperate Sam was, she decided to ask the director if the search operation could be extended for a few more hours. The director agreed. And the search and rescue crew got ready for one last search, and they all returned to the airfield. Every nook and cranny was checked again. As the search was being conducted, Sam suddenly realized that they should also check the outer parameters of the airfield as well as its outer edges. Along with some of the members of the crew, Sam and Jane went out.

They searched every tunnel and circled the entirety of the outer parameters and found nothing. They returned empty-handed. But while returning, Sam suddenly saw a slight movement under a pile of rubble. He immediately shouted, "Guys, I see some movement there, under that pile of rocks."

Everyone rushed and they too saw it move. One of the students said, "I had looked here. The area the rubble is covering up seemed rather small. I didn't think a person could fit underneath. So I didn't unearth it."

They all started digging through the rubble carefully. After a few rocks had been removed, they could see the legs of a person. They cleared the remaining rubble and found a boy inside it. He could fit inside such a small area because he had crawled into a foetal position, in the shape of a semi-circle when the rubble had fallen on him. He was alive.

Everyone began to acknowledge Sam for having extended the search and helping them save yet another person, who would have otherwise been forgotten. Jane turned to Sam and said, "How do you have such strong feelings? You are always right when you say you feel something."

"I guess I am special." He smiled back at Jane.

The guy they found there was Krisden, a medical science student. He had severe head injuries and many of his bones were broken, but the rubble on top of him had actually saved him from the fire.

Sam and Jane were joined by Kasmuji as they came out of the airfield. Kasmuji was quick to ask, "Sam, Jane, how did you guys manage to end up on the other side of the fence?"

Sam and Jane told him about how everything: how they had ended up at the tunnel, the flood, how they decided to go to the other side of it, and about the saw-like grass. As they were talking, they got into the vehicle that was to take them to the Dorm.

The convoy of the vehicles carrying some of the injured, and the members of the search and rescue team, flew off from the site towards Volgarth. The injured were first taken to the Medical Center at Volgarth for primary treatment and their families were informed. Sam and Jane, along with the remaining students who were not harmed significantly in the fire, were sent back to the Dorm. They were asked to go to their rooms and rest. Volgarth was still on high alert.

The good news was that most of the students had already left when the explosions occurred, and the fatality rate was relatively low at 10 percent. Grief and sorrow had engulfed Volgarth. Sam and Jane were still shocked by the sights of the debris, Kasmuji and the other staff of Volgarth were still busy trying to find anyone who requires help. They were working to provide every available support to the injured and consoling the loved ones of those who lost their lives. The atmosphere in the Dorm was tensed. On the one hand, there was the grief of losing friends, and on the other, there was restlessness to help the ones in need. For the first time, the corridors of the dorm lay vacant and silence engulfed the dorm. The night seemed darker than usual and the wind was still.

But the job of the Volgarth authorities had just begun. An emergency committee was set up that very night to investigate into the matter. All the teachers were included in the committee.

At the first meeting of the committee, the director said, "Today has been one of the darkest days at Volgarth. We failed to protect our own children. We have set up this committee to look up into the matter. We need answers as to whether the explosion took place due to a technical fault or if it was a well-executed plan. If a plan, then you all know what is coming. We need to learn about it as soon as possible. Also, help from various planets and the IMMR will be arriving early tomorrow. We need to stick together in this dire situation, and we have to rebuild this place from what is left. I urge all of you to cooperate with one another and find answers that will help us. Volgarth is not going to sleep for some days."

Each member of the committee was given specific responsibilities. At the end of the meeting, when all dispersed to fulfil the tasks that they had been assigned, the director asked Kasmuji to stay. Closing the door, he said, "Kasmuji, you know that if this was a well-executed plan, it's because of that boy—Sam. His life will be in danger. You must keep an eye on him. You do understand what I am saying, don't you?"

Kasmuji nodded and said, "Don't worry, sir. I won't let anything happen to him. I already told you—if we could find him, so will the others. But, don't worry, I won't let him out of my sight."

Saying that he left the room. The director continued to sit in his chair, concerned about the future.

There were lights all over Volgarth. The pillars, the Dorm, even the road beside the wall had been covered in light. Special guards had already been called for and would be arriving the next day. The ancient text on the walls had been covered. The magical elements at Volgarth were hidden from sight, and all the labs were sealed, and all secret doors were closed. Travel was only allowed using a vehicle that moved from one part of the area to another. Staff was sent to the airfield to clear space for the spaceships that were to land the very next day. A temporary control unit was set up. The emergency arrangements continued through the night.

Sam lay on his bed. As he opened his eyes, he could see the light drift in through the window. He jumped out of his bed, and realizing that it was morning, was fast to get freshened up and out. He desperately wanted to know what had happened through the night. When he reached the ground floor, the other students were already here. As he walked through the crowd, he saw Jane. As he went near her, John, Mariane, Jonathan, Jason, Juliana, Partick, and Indiana were also there. He could not believe his eyes. He immediately walked up to them and asked, "What are you guys doing here?"

Jane had already told them everything that happened. They knew how Sam had saved Jane. She also told them how Sam's instincts had helped them save the life of Krisden. They all noticed his bandages and empathized with what he had gone through. John hugged Sam and said, "As soon as we heard about what happened here, we were terrified. We knew that you and Jane were still here. So we tried to contact Jane's house, and they told us that both of you were still here, and were safe. We wanted to see for ourselves. We all contacted each other and came back. We cannot express how happy we are to see both of you. You both scared us a lot, you know."

By that time, everybody had come around and was busy hugging Sam and Jane. The wolf pack was together again. Sam felt so happy, finally, after so many years, he had people who cared about him, who would go the mile to ensure his well-being. There were tears in his eyes. He held everyone tightly. Even in situations like these, their friendship had held strong.

Help from the other planets and the IMMR had already arrived by then. The families of those injured had also arrived. The injured were taken away from Volgarth so they could receive advanced health care. Sam and the wolf pack decided to go and see what state the airfield was is. They boarded a vehicle and asked to be taken there. Upon reaching, they saw spacecraft unloading materials for the planet, and Special Guards patrolling the entire area. So many of them were there. They carried in relief materials and carried away injured students.

However, the airfield less busy than what it had been a day before. Still, the hustle was palpable. They approached a gate. The Special Guards who had been posted there prohibited them from entering the airfield, citing many reasons, but they were insistent. Just then, the director happened to pass by the area. On seeing the director, the students shouted out, seeking his special permission. The director nodded and asked the guards to let them in and they thanked him profusely.

The wolf pack looked around at the devastation that had been caused. Burned buildings, piles of rubble and debris. Sam and Jane were shocked to see that the smoke had dissipated, and all was clear within a night.

As they were looking around, Mr Gregor walked up behind them and said, "Look, we have visitors. How are you, Sam and Jane?"

Sam and Jane turned to him and said, "We are fine, sir. We are surprised to see how everything has transformed within a night."

Mr Gregor smiled and said, "This is how things work here. We could not keep idle, thinking about all that has happened to us. We must stand up, and together do away with the wrongs that plague us, with determination. We are all tested from time to time. The outcome depends on us—do we face the situation, or sit and blame our luck? Moreover, thanks to you Sam, we have fewer fatalities despite such an accident. We could have had a lot more than 10 percent of our students as victims of this grimly incident."

These words brought relief to Sam's face. As they were talking to Mr Gregor, they saw the entire emergency committee heading their way. They stopped when they saw Mr Gregor and spoke to him about sending the students home.

In the middle of their discussion, Sam interrupted, "Sir, I would like to stay here and help in rebuilding the academy."

Everyone stopped talking and gaped at Sam. Kasmuji finally spoke.

"Sam, it may not be safe for you here. You saw what happened here yesterday. We cannot risk having any student here."

Sam did not want to agree and said, "Nothing will happen to us here. We even have the Special Guards with us now. Please allow me to stay and help. Moreover, I don't have anyone else to go home to. This is my home, and I really want to stay."

Hearing Sam say this, the other students of the wolf pack also insisted that they be allowed to stay. They all wanted to help the institute. None of them wanted to leave for a vacation at this point. They kept pleading that they be allowed to stay. They even troubled the director and sought permission directly from him. At last, the director agreed, "Okay, you all will be allowed to stay. But we must first get letters of permission from your parents. After what has happened here, I will not keep you here without your parents' permission. Get me that and you can stay."

The director paused and looked at Sam guiltily. Sam interjected immediately, "Don't worry sir; I am not offended at all. But this means that I can surely stay, right?"

The director nodded with a smile.

The students went to call and get their letters of permission. Most of their parents refused, concerned about their well-being. Only Jason, Jonathan, John, and Juliana were able to convince their parents. The rest of had to go. With heavy hearts, they packed again and got ready. They bid the ones who were staying back a warm farewell and wished them well.

Sam, John, Jonathan, Jason, and Juliana were the only ones left behind. They knew that they have to work as hard with the other staff there. As their friends went off in their spacecraft again, they stood there, excited about the adventures to come their way.

CHAPTER 9

First Voyage

After the incident that shook the entire institution, Volgarth finally moved on. The staff worked round the clock to rebuild the airfield. Sam and the wolf pack also played their part. As the second term began at Volgarth, the emergency committee was still investigating the issue. According to their reports, it was found that the LMV, which was the first to explode, did not have any passengers. As most LMV's were remotely operated, this was entirely possible. However, according to reports from the control rooms, the LMV was seen to be *taking off* from Tiron, not *landing*. Under normal circumstances, an empty LMV would never have taken off. Since LMV's are programmed to be very efficient and timely, if its passengers had not arrived at the stipulated time, it would be assigned elsewhere. Further investigations revealed that that particular LMV was a dual passenger type. Such small LMVs were used only to travel long distances. All these things caused the investigation to come to halt. The committee did not know what exactly these investigations would achieve, but they kept at it. It was decided that the investigation would be carried out alongside normal activities at Volgarth. The director asked that it be kept a secret.

The classes for the second term had started. This was when most students conducted their first field trips. The students would be taken to various planets where the IMMR was conducting their research. The IMMR provided the necessary resources to researchers who wanted to take the quest to find the magical world further.

Over the years, the IMMR had found several manuscripts, maps, fossils, spacecraft remains and more on various planets in the universe, which indicated that long before, a magical world existed, but for some reason, it had disappeared. Finding such a world would mean gaining access to immense powers and controlling the entire universe. However, the IMMR wanted to find that world and contain its powers for the benefits of the universe. They wanted to find the answers to the questions that remained a mystery for humanity. But another institution, known as Universal Association of Deceased Men (UADM), a group of the most notorious criminals of the universe existed at the same time. It was headed by Grisken. Grisken was considered to be the maddest criminal mind to have ever been born in the history of humanity. He was not strong, but he was a genius. He had been associated with numerous criminal activities across the universe such as smuggling of illegal items, assassinations, the sale of weapons of mass destruction, stealing from the governments of different planets, planting bombs, kidnapping, blackmailing and much more. He was associated with all kinds of crimes in the universe, starting from the tiniest crime to the most severe evil. Being a genius, he had built his own spacecraft and was also associated with the manufacturing of deadly weapons. He was funded by several strange rich men. He was very smart, and no government in the universe could even catch him. Universal Police (UNIPOL) had placed a bounty on his head.

Grisken was also a thinker and had a curious mind. He had always been interested in the magical world, aware of the powers it could bring into his life. He learnt of it when he had stumbled across a manuscript in a planet that he had gone to rob. He took that manuscript to the illegal markets, and there, someone translated the manuscript for him. The manuscript outlined the existence of such a world, millions of years ago, and its sudden disappearance from the universe. From that day on, he kept a close eye on Volgarth and the IMMR as they were institutions that could further his own quest.

He formed the institution, UADM, bringing in criminal minds from all over the universe. He freed many prisoners from various planets and asked them to join his group. He funded the group with his own money. And this illustrious gang also started to look for the magical world. Besides their quest of finding the magical world, the group also continued to indulge in various criminal activities. It was believed that Grisken had provided powers to each member of his group by altering their genes, or implanting chips under their skin, or replacing parts of their bodies with technological devices. The explosion at Volgarth was thought to be the handiwork of Grisken.

The researchers at the IMMR were used to problems faced due to the extreme working conditions, but now they were faced with a very different kind of problem in the form of Grisken.

On the very first day of class in the second term, the students briefed on Grisken. Volgarth and the IMMR wanted its students to know that they had to find the magical world before Grisken would. Or else, the universe and its entire species would be at the mercy of that evil mastermind. The class was taken by Mr Esdorg.

"Where there is good, there will be evil. You must do everything you can to find the magical world before them, and at the same time, you must do everything in your power to stop UADM. Your second term starts now. Tomorrow, all of you will be sent on your first field training. You have already been assigned groups, with whom you have stayed and conducted many activities together in your first term. However, I don't know how many of you remember, the director said in his speech on your first day, that although you are assigned specific groups, you will get the opportunity to work with members of other groups. So, for your field visits, you will be assigned different groups. You are requested to come one by one and collect your group numbers."

The students collected their group numbers and the groups were formed accordingly. Sam, Jane, and Jonathan formed one group. Mariane was with Juliana and Patrick. John's group had Jason and Indiana. Although they had been separated from each other, the wolf pack was still together. All its members now formed one large group. The students were relieved of their classes that day and were asked to prepare. They were not informed where they would be taken the following day.

As the students left, Mr Gregor came in and gestured that he wanted a word with Mr Esdorg. Standing in a dark corner, he said, "It's good that the students are going ahead. Volgarth may not be as safe for them yet."

Mr Esdorg nodded his assent and said, "We have a lot of work to do in the meantime."

It was time for everyone to go forward into their first voyage into the unknown. Their spacecraft arrived and everybody boarded them. They were taken together to the planets. There, the groups assigned to the particular planets, would be sent to their respective sites through space pods. It was possible that more than one group was assigned to a planet, depending upon the number of the IMMR sites on that planet. However, it was made sure, that if more than one group was on a planet, their positions had to be far away from each other.

John and his group were being sent to a planet called Desertoin. It was a desert planet. However, it had many reservoirs of water underneath it, as well as clues regarding the magical world buried in its bed. It especially had many ruins of spacecraft, dating back to millions of years. Mariane and her group were sent to a planet called Kepler112, a planet discovered when humans had just learnt to set foot on space. This planet now served as one of the most important sources of medical inventions and many fossils of mysterious creatures had been unearthed here. Both these planets were full of ancient manuscripts and also had human-resembling skeletal remains on them. Many groups of students were sent to the bases located at various points on those planets.

Sam and his group were sent to a planet called Dirthron. They were sent on their pods to the IMMR base there. On their way, they could not see any other pods landing. They believed that they were the only ones assigned to Dirthron.

They reached the base and were received by the head, Mr Ravi. Mr Ravi was a tall figure with a moustache and a muscular build. He welcomed them and introduced himself, after which they were shown to their rooms. After some time, Mr Ravi came to take them around the facility on a guided tour of the work that was being done there.

Mr Ravi introduced them to the other working staff there. There were also students from the previous batches of Volgarth working there now. The facility was large and contained many pieces of complex machinery, many of which Sam and his group recognized from their first-term classes. They were astonished to see such a huge facility working for the discovery of the magical world. And they realized how significant their cause was, that they were a part of something big.

Mr Ravi decided he would tell the group about the planet first and briefly explain why it was an important research site. He said that Dirthron was inhabited by various species of animals and plants. The animals and plants found there were very dangerous. The animals very small in size but were equipped with dangerous poisons. Most of the plants too were poisonous. He told them that if they were to touch the bark of a tree; the poison would diffuse into their body and could be fatal. He further said, "When this planet was first discovered in the early stages of space exploration, it seemed very suited for life. The air was breathable, the gravity was suitable, it had water, minerals—everything necessary for life was here. Plans were then made to colonize this planet, but no presence of any intelligent species was found on this planet."

were sent to learn about the place, and to hunt for suitable habitats. They had no idea what lay on this planet. When the first space traveller came, they landed near a lake and decided to camp near it. They put up their tents and went on to see the planet's beauty. They tested the water and the air and found it to be suitable. Although the planet had a safe amount of air, they did not take off their suits and continued their expedition. They went inside the vast forests to collect some plant samples. Inside the jungle, they found many species of insects and small animals. They took a few of them back. On their way back, one of the space travellers noticed that some small insects were inside his suit, and immediately after, he fell to the ground, dead. The others had no idea what had happened to him. They cut open his suit. And, thousands of small insects emerged from it. The other travellers then knew that something was wrong with the planet. The insects looked harmless enough, but they had done something to their mate. They immediately collected the samples of as many kinds of living thing they could see and flew off immediately."

"What happened next?" the students asked. A sense of desperateness could be seen in their faces.

Mr Ravi continued …

"Back at the research facility, it was found that the space traveller had died due to a deadly poison. The samples that were brought back were tested, and it was found that every plant and every insect that the space travellers had brought contained the same poison that had killed the space traveller."

"Was the water of Dirthron contaminated too by the poison?" Jonathan asked.

To this, Mr Ravi responded, "The soil and water samples brought were however free from any kind of contamination and were of good quality and could support life. The scientists at the research facility could not understand the reason for such an anomaly, and they contacted the IMMR. Back then, the IMMR was a deep space exploration facility, which explored the universe in search of minerals and Quanta. It was known as QSEA. Quanta was a newly discovered element at the time. The huge power requirement of this universe is now fulfilled by Quanta, as you all should know. The IMMR first started its journey as QSEA to find Quanta among the various planets in the universe. It was an extremely rare element then. QSEA was known to have developed very advanced machinery for space exploration. So Dirthron was given to QSEA for further exploration. When our first exploration team reached here, they knew one thing—all the plants, trees, insects, and other smaller animals were poisonous, and they had to be very careful."

"What did the exploration team find out in Dirthron?" Jane asked at this point.

Mr Ravi replied, "During their exploration, they found fossils of some very ancient creatures. Skeletal structures they had never seen. From their research, they found that the fossils, however, did not have any poison affecting their DNA, unlike what had been seen in the present living beings on that planet. They deduced that life on the planet had not always been the same. After exploring this planet, QSEA declared it unfit for colonization, but as they were about to leave the planet, one of the explorers found that the planet's core was rich in minerals not known to humankind, including a huge resource of Quanta. QSEA conveyed this message to the authorities and asked permission to look for Quanta here. This is when this facility was set up to provide a safe working experience for the researchers, away from the poisonous environment outside."

As Mr Ravi continued, Sam asked, "Sir, did you find Quanta here, and how does this planet serve the purpose of finding the magical world?"

Mr Ravi replied, "For the first few years, QSEA extracted an abundant amount of Quanta from this planet. By that time, the idea of the magical world had come into existence inside QSEA. Initial research had already started. In the course of digging for Quanta, we found evidence of superior life in Dirthron. The fossils were only the start. Upon close inspection, it was found that beneath the reserves of Quanta, there was a hollow space. The problem was, in order to reach that place, the Quanta had to be completely extracted. Despite their valiant efforts, it was not possible to dig through the Quanta to reach the hollow space. Extracting the Quanta was also difficult. This planet has provided us with more Quanta than any other planet till now. There is still a 1 cm thick layer of Quanta on top of the hollow space, prohibiting us from reaching there. By now, QSEA had become the IMMR, and after much research, we now know that some kind of magic is holding down that layer of Quanta. We believe this planet was witness to one of the grimmest wars in the history of the universe. As we dug around this planet, we found more and more fossils. We also found some human skeletal remains, and some from a lesser developed species, which dated back millions of years. This changed our perception of this planet. We discovered that beneath the green surface of this planet lies a battlefield. Thousands and thousands of fossils recovered from this place are being researched. The most shocking fact about this planet was remains of spacecraft, which were much more powerful than the conventional spacecraft we use today. The Mach Light spacecraft that were recently discovered were built by studying the remains of the spacecraft we found here. Humans and other intelligent species possessing such technology millions of years ago had earlier seemed impossible. This has only made our belief in the existence of magic and the Creators much stronger. Research on one of the skeletal structures indicated that their DNA was the oldest to be ever found."

Mr Ravi took them to a highly automated research facility within the main facility, "This is where we have kept most of the fossils and research is conducted here." He pointed towards a fossil and said, "This is the skeleton of the fossil I was talking about. As you can see, its skeletal structure is less evolved than that of a human, but we have found from their DNA that they were a species whose lifespan was very long, and from their skull, we can say that this was a species whose brain size grew with age. All these observations confused us, until we discovered a manuscript about the history of humanity and the wars of the universe from another distant planet. From that manuscript, we now believe that these are the remains of Resgords, and this planet may be Emphor."

As soon as Mr Ravi said these words, Sam, Jane, and Jonathan stood still and looked aghast at each other. The story Mr Gregor had told them about! Resgords and the planet Emphor! They had goosebumps at that moment. They knew that whatever had been taught were actual facts.

Mr Ravi continued and said, 'So, you guys have a lot to learn from this place. Jane, you have to study these fossils, Jonathan, you have to study the machines here. They are the most important component of our research, and you will be working to keep them up and running. Sam, you will have to try and find a way through that magical 1 cm layer of Quanta. You will have much more freedom than the rest of the two. You might even have to leave the planet to find your answers. You have to use everything you have learnt, and most importantly, you have to believe. So, are you all ready for the adventure to come?"

His cheeks broadened with an honest smile.